Praise for *THE BOY WHO MADE IT RAIN*

"innovative and insightful novel... I couldn't wait to devour part two..."

Sue Palmer, *Times Educational Supplement*

*

"I was utterly flabbergasted. I began reading it early in the morning and I didn't put it down until I had finished it that evening... this is perhaps one of the most compelling novels I've ever read"

Heffers Review, Cambridge

*

"one of the most skilfully written that we have read in a long, time... not so much a summer read as a must read – definitely up there with the modern classics"

What? Magazine

*

"A must-read for teens and adults... an innovative novel that will keep you glued to the story until you turn the last page and learn the final outcome..."

Fran Lewis: *New York Reviewer, educator and talk-show host and interviewer*

*

Brian Conaghan

The Boy Who
Made it Rain

Sparkling Books

The right of Brian Conaghan to be identified as the author of this work has been asserted by him in accordance with the Copyright, Designs and Patents Act 1988.

This book is a work of fiction. Names, characters, businesses, organisations, places, events and incidents are either the products of the author's imagination or are used fictitiously. Any resemblance to actual persons, living or dead, events or places is entirely coincidental.

British Library Cataloguing in Publication Data. A catalogue record for this book is available from the British Library.

Cover image © istockphoto.com/Bodhi Hill

1.4

Recommended age: 16+

ISBN: 978-1-907230-19-6

Edited by Anna Alessi.

First published in paperback in June 2011.

Printed in the United Kingdom by Good News Digital Books.

For more information visit *www.sparklingbooks.com*

Education is like a double-edged sword. It may be turned to dangerous uses if it is not properly handled.

Wu Ting-Fang

For Orla

A huge hug goes out to my friends and family. A special thanks to Anna Alessi and everyone at Sparkling Books for their support, encouragement and belief throughout this process and, of course, to all the school kids I have taught over the years, without whom this book would never have been written.

Part One

What They Said

Rosie Farrell's First Impression

We met when Clem first came to our school. It was two weeks into term. He was from somewhere down in the south of England. I don't know. I'd never heard of the place. Still haven't, even though he told me about it loads of times. Sounds rubbish wherever it is though. He had a funny accent, that's why everyone sort of fancied him. Including most of the *out* guys. Cora said he had that Robbie Williams thing going on…all the guys wanted to be him and all the girls wanted to…well, you know. He didn't say much at first; just did his work and kept his head down. Bore a minute.

Yes, he was smart. Dead smart. He'd read all these things that we couldn't even pronounce, all this foreign stuff. Get a life, right? But he wasn't a big-headed bragger or anything like that. I wasn't much of a reader so I thought I was well out of his league. Not that I really wanted to be in it in the first place. I usually find all that stuff dead boring. Reading and all that.

English was his thing though; he sat down the front like a pure teacher's pet. He was into challenging them all the time. The teachers. Having all these debates about dead dull stuff. Nonsense. Boreathon, right? I thought Miss Croal flirted with him from day one. She was one of those fresh-out-of-training-college teachers. And they're all the same. They come breezing in with heads full of Hollywood films and a desire to 'make a difference.' Airheads with no clue whatsoever. To tell you the truth it was kind of embarrassing watching her make an eejit out of herself. Revelling in thinking she was this kind of fountain of knowledge. Fountain of lavvy water more like!

Honestly, Miss Croal was as bright as a blackout. No, I didn't take the mickey. Not my style, I'm a passive observer. Yes, some people did. But not bullying or intimidation, or anything like that. Well, it's a bit of a red neck, but my friend Cora used to say *Miss Croal's gagging for her hole* when she started flirting and flicking the eyes to all the guys. Once she actually said it to her face, but in rhyming slang.

She said, erm, *gantin for your Nat King, Miss?* Croal would never have guessed what it meant. She was probably from the posh part of town. The West End or something.

She was like that, Cora, real brash, in your face stuff. But she was a howl.

Yes, he was different from the other guys and not just because he was clever, or good-looking. Well, he wasn't good-looking in a conventional sense, but he could've definitely been one of those *Benetton* models. You know, the ones who are borderline ugly. That's what Cora thought anyway. There were loads of girls who thought he was like all Mr Mysterious, but to me he was more like Mr Weirdo. I said to Cora that there was something no right about him, like concealing a secret or something. Sometimes I'd catch him staring right at me, not in a freak-show way, more in a crying-out-for-a-friend way.

Was I popular? When I was in fifth-year all the fifth- and sixth-years kept asking me out. I kept telling them to blow town. Which is a way of saying go away. Or rather Cora did on my behalf. None of them did anything for me. I snogged a couple of them but nothing beyond that. Or enough to get the heart cartwheeling. I wouldn't have gone that far with the guys at my school. No way. So, yes you could say that I was popular, but I wasn't a bitch or anything like that...it wasn't like *The O.C.* it was real life, and we were into keeping it real. *Real* real not in the rap way. I had friends from all the groups. Apart from the NEDs that is...Up here we call them NEDs... means Non Educated Delinquents. Could be a lot worse I suppose, like TITs...Total Idiot Thickos.

He was just different...well...because...because...well for a start, he had an accent. Anyone who had a different accent was automatically deemed to be cool. It's a sort of unwritten law in schools, isn't it? I mean if I went to an American school I'd be fighting them off with a big stick. He said words like girl and film without pronouncing the R or L properly. Gewl. It was kind of cute. And then there was his name. Most guys here are bogged down in all this I-want-to-be-Irish guff. Just because they were seventeenth generation Irish, or something like that, they all thought they were pure dead Irish. I mean, get a life! I blame their parents. Look around, everyone's called Liam, Keron, Conor, Sean, Niall or some other duff Irish name. It's really boring and predictable. So when we first heard the name Clem we thought it was pure hilarious. Then we realised that the name Clem made him sort of stand out from all the Irish wannabes. It was bomb how his name had that whole alliteration thing going on as well, Clem Curran. You know, C and C. That's one thing I can thank Miss Croal for. I'm not exactly like Shakespeare at English but she explained what alliteration was by using his name as an example, that's how it sunk in. When I'm an old woman, forty or fifty or something, and I hear the word *alliteration* I'll automatically say 'Clem Curran' in my head. 'Cool Clem

Curran' I said to Cora. 'Classy Cora and Cool Clem Curran cruising and kissing in a convertible coupe' she said back. I don't think kissing counts but. Suppose that was the start of it. No, it was that badge.

I had a *Bright Eyes* badge on my bag. Not the wee rabbits! *Bright Eyes*, the band. They were my favourites at that time. Not now. I still like them and all, but you know what young people are like. We change our favourite things from one week to the next. From one day to the next. Anyway, I was listening to loads of *Bright Eyes* stuff, couldn't get enough of them. So I went out and bought some badges for my bag. You know this fad with bags full of badges? I was tapping into it. If my mum put badges on her bags I'd be pure morto... Mortified.

Right, so me and Clem were partnered together in our Italian class to do some role-play stuff about tourists asking for directions in Rome, or somewhere like that. I mean, when will that ever come in handy? Don't get me started on language classes at our school. Anyway we were giving it all the 'you need to go straight down the road and turn left then take the first right and then you will see the Spanish Steps' jargon, all in Italian of course, when he clocks the *Bright Eyes* badge on my bag.

'I didn't know you were an emo chick', he said.

I said, 'who are you calling a flippin emu? And never call me a chick again.'

I didn't actually say the word flippin, did I?

Then when he told me what emo meant I felt like a total

Paris. Then we had a conversation about music and school and students and teachers and just general angsty teenager car-crash stuff. He had some good chat. He told me where he was from, but it sounded too dull so we spoke about me. When I went home that night I was thinking about him loads and the next day I sort of fancied him.

I'd just then discovered *The Smiths*.

Cora Kelly's Opinion

Oh my God! It's not as if I fancied Clem or anything. Rosie's a pure liar if she said that. I can't believe people would even think that. That's a pure riot. We spoke about him:

A. Coz he was new to the school

and

B. Coz that's what we do when chatting about the guys.

All girls do that. You should hear what they say about us, by the way. Someone put it around that I gave this wee third-year a five-ten-double-ten after the third-year disco…A hand jive…you know, pulled him off. Then I heard all these wee third-years whispering to each other in the corridor. So I went to the guy with the motor gub and said that I'd boot his nose through his ear if he didn't say it was a load of crap. Let's say he quickly took it all back. I mean, why would I turn up at a third-year disco in the first place? I'm not into jigging away to *The Jonas Brothers* thank you very much. What I'm saying is don't believe everything you hear in here that's all. All it takes is one text message and the next thing you're the biggest slut in the whole school. Sometimes I wish I could go back to the olden days when they didn't have mobiles. My mum still talks about those days. Can you imagine it but? You'd be pure Billy No Mates.

Actually Rosie knew that I sort of fancied Conor Duffy. Even though he was into like football and all that male bonding crap, which is way uncool. I still liked him. Away from his pals he was actually okay. I could just about stomach all that *hail! hail! the Celts are here* drivel but there's no way I could've put up with all that we're-from-the-hood mince. Yeah right, in Glasgow? And you should hear the way they talk, as if they're from the manky part of town, with that pure cartoon Glasgow accent. It's totally put on coz I've heard the way some of them talk to their mums, and it's a billion miles from what comes out their traps in school. But I definitely drew the line at all the hip-hop singing and references. I mean have you heard *50Cent* and *JayZ* done in a Scottish accent? Sounds like an idiot with a speech impediment. I still liked him though.

It's like one of those guilty…thingymajigs…pleasures, that's right. A guilty pleasure. Rosie said he was a bit of a tosser, so I tried not to like him. No, I don't always do what Rosie tells me to do. You listen to your mates, don't you? I'm not hiding stuff here.

Clem?

Clem was okay, in a boring I'm-into-books-and-reading-all-the-time type of way. He had a funny name and a funny accent. Some girls are attracted to all that. They were all saying he was the spit of some guy from *The OC* but I never watch *The OC* so I couldn't really say. Too much teeth for my liking. To me it was like listening to someone off *Eastenders* or *Hollyoaks*. That's the most erotic it gets here…No, I don't mean that…Different, that's all…Exotic then. Erotic exotic same thing.

After about a week in school he had everyone eating out the palm of his hand. I called it the Robbie Williams effect. You know, all the guys want to…how do you know? Anyway there were some girls, especially in the year below, who were slobbering whenever he passed by them in the corridor, like they were at some *JLS* music store gig. It was pathetic. Believe it or not Miss Croal was the worst though.

She was practically salivating every time he came into her English class. Even I was embarrassed for her. No, I never gave her a hard time over it…well, maybe the odd wee comment here or there…nothing nasty.

Sometimes these new teachers need to be put in their place. It happens to them all. They're all full of innovation. It's so annoying. I mean, just give us a book and let us read it, or we'll pretend we're reading it. We don't have to examine what every blinking word means. I didn't even want to do English, it's not like I was going to do it as a career or anything like that. It's a boring head wreck. Worse than going to the school mass. I still look in the dictionary for swear words in English class to keep it exciting, that's how bad it is. Why do schools force everybody to do it? It doesn't make any sense. I say let all the nerds do it if they want and let the rest of us do extra classes on the subjects we enjoy…I sort of wanted to be a vet, but I'm mince at Biology and I don't really like the sight of blood. But I do like animals…who knows, maybe I'll do a drama course or something, I don't know yet. My guidance teacher suggested beauty therapy, and I was like: Christ on a bike, Sir, I'm not *that* thick.

It was kind of worrying when Clem came to the school coz I was worried that me and Rosie would both fancy him and there would be this pure tension between us, so I tried dead hard not to fancy him. Then when I heard him talking all that rubbish in the English class I knew that I could never fancy him. Not my type, you see. I reckon he must have been a Libran or something, coz Sagittarians and Librans can't stand each other. Or is it Leos? Whatever he was, I could tell that we were totally out of sync. But I could tell that Rosie liked him. She was like pure rash material always looking at him when he wasn't looking and going all red and shy when he was about. For a time I thought she was going to turn into some mad-stalker bird. Thing is, Rosie could have gotten any guy in the school. All of fifth- and sixth-year guys thought she was a ride. She didn't cake herself in make-up like most of the dogs in fifth- and sixth-year, who thought they were pure God's gift. That's the thing about Rosie, she didn't know how good-looking she was.

I wasn't jealous...why would I be jealous? I had loads of guys chasing me. Even guys with cars and guys who were, like, working. I could hold my own. I didn't want a bf... boyfriend. I couldn't be arsed with all that 'childhood sweet-hearts' crap. It's not as if I was a slapper or anything like that, I just didn't want the hassle of a bf. No way. Stuff that! Half the girls from third-year up are probably on the pill so it's no great surprise. In fact, if you believe any of the stories in this place, half of the lassies in our year have probably been marched down to the abortion clinic at one time or another while the other half pop the morning-after pill as if they're Tic-Tacs. I was always careful. It's not like it's the eighties we're in. Anyway me and Rosie were totally different, not just in looks, for a start she was into all that oh-I'm-dead-depressed-I'm-going-to-slit-my-wrists music. She tried for ages to get me into it but it just made me want to self harm. I need beats and rhythm. Even if I wanted to I could never have

11

fancied Clem; I'd never have done anything to hurt Rosie. She was my best pal.

Of course I'm shocked...

Am I sad? That's another thing, isn't it?

Pauline Croal's Understanding

It was my first position out of teacher training college so naturally I approached the job with a great deal of enthusiasm. I also had a duty to my students to engage them in the subject. Long gone are the days of the antiquated practice of teaching from the board or enforcing individual study throughout the duration of the lesson. I did try to be more innovative and foster an environment more conducive to the learning process. It's also what we were encouraged to do at college. After all, it's the reason I entered the profession.

No, I didn't find the school that difficult. Obviously I had no point of reference, however, I am led to believe from various members of staff that it was a tolerable school to work in. My own schooling wasn't that far removed from my teaching experience there. The school was full of characters. I liked that. Both students and staff alike. It's fair to say that some older members of staff didn't like their feathers being ruffled; they prefer to exist in the malaise. All that stereotypical stuff we are warned about as students, coffee mugs and specific seats belonging to certain teachers are all true. A solid phalanx of hostility was apparent. There is a definite hierarchy in school staffrooms. A few months of observing the political situations, I found it stuffy and embittered. There seemed no desire to embrace change; too many teachers were set in their ways, waiting for the bells to ring, for the summer to come around. There was also the cynicism that grated on me. Lots of my colleagues had nothing positive to say about the students they taught. To be honest I was a touch surprised by the sheer disregard and contempt they had for their profession. In any other industry they would have been sacked. However many teachers simply close their doors and exercise a methodology that has no place in modern education practice. It's too difficult to sack teachers these days. You have to cross a particular threshold for that to happen...I am babbling. I have a tendency to do that.

Obviously I am aware that this is a generalisation because not all teachers were like this. Some of us cared. I cared about my students and I invested in them. I endeavoured to encourage and cajole my students into developing a love for my subject. No, it didn't always work.

I suppose that's teaching for you. It could be said that I used my students as a solace from the challenges of the staffroom. They were my escape. I was continuously alert to the fact that I wouldn't allow the passion and fervour I showed for my subject to be misconstrued or misinterpreted. I was always aware of that. It's every teacher's nightmare. I was no different in that respect.

It was like any other fifth- and sixth-year class, some showed a real desire for English, others apathy, some quiet and unassuming while others were boisterous. Just your average classroom gene pool. Rosie Farrell? There was nothing that struck me as odd about Rosie; your typical senior-year girl, full of teenage angst and misplaced rebellion. She had a thing about me...that's not what I mean.

I mean she was distant and resentful for some reason. We didn't really develop much of a teacher/student relationship it has to be said. I had the impression that she felt that I had a different agenda other than that of getting them involved in the subject and success in their exam, which was in fact my only agenda. I have no idea whatsoever why she felt this way. I certainly wasn't going to challenge a sixteen-year-old girl on such matters. After all, I was the one who was in the position of responsibility. I had to show maturity, leadership and integrity; confronting a student simply because you have a distinct feeling that that student doesn't like you is unprofessional and short-sighted. I am afraid I wasn't that insecure about myself, or my methods, either.

Having said that, my understanding was that Rosie was a clever girl, sharp as a tac as well. I believed that she was more than capable of achieving anything she wanted to achieve. Actually I liked her individuality, or her desire to be individual. She seemingly didn't subscribe to what her peers were interested in. As regards her dress sense, the music she listened to or her general attitude, she was what you would call an emo girl. Which means emotional. It's related to that type of music. Emotional music, I'd imagine. It goes further than that, obviously, in the sense that it's linked to the general aesthetic and attitude. Iconoclastic, and subversive with a small 's'. Rosie certainly fell into that category; she was a fusion of these things. It's not as though we teachers don't listen to music. It should be a prerequisite that we have to garner knowledge of popular culture. If anything we are more attuned to teenagers than any other profession. I'd advise all teachers to watch the X Factor, Big Brother or The Inbetweeners. It's about trying to engage. It's not rocket science, you know.

Rosie had a flair for English; however, I don't think she could comprehend this. At times it's tough to be objective, to have that ability to stand outside yourself and analyse successes and areas for improvement. Maybe that's where teachers come in handy. I could tell that she had real potential. My understanding was that she enjoyed *Macbeth* and some of Shakespeare's sonnets.

I thought Cora Kelly was a noose around Rosie's neck. It was obvious that she was a bad influence on her; perhaps it was based on some intellectual inferiority complex or, indeed, a visual one. You know how teenage girls can be. I understood there to be a hint of resentment within that friendship. Cora could be an odious character, but there was something charmingly heartbreaking about her at the same time. She required an audience; if Rosie wasn't in class for whatever reason Cora was like a morose dog without its owner. There was something more profound going on with that girl. None of my colleagues had a good word to say about her, but please don't take that as any kind of barometer. There was no way on earth that she was going to pass her exam. Why? Simply because she was weak, and indolent. I think it was suggested to her that she was maybe better off leaving school and enrolling in the local technical college to study beauty therapy. In my mind it was a good idea. I am not sure why she didn't; my theory is that she enjoyed the comforts, camaraderie and security that school provided her with.

Clem Curran? Well, that's the story, isn't it?

Conor Duffy's Insightfulness

He spoke dead posh man. An that name, what's that all aboot? Did his maw an da no like him or somethin? He couldnay understan half the things we said, which made chattin a nightmare. Coz we wir the senior guys we wir asked to show him the ropes, like aroon the school and in the common room an that. Tell him the unofficial rules an codes an all that.

Where the smokers' area wiz.

Where you could dogg it in the school withoot gettin caught.

Who wir the good teachers an who wir the drongos. The clowns.

What students wir alright to hing way an who wir the total nerds an geeks.

Who the maddies wir.

Aye, the students who we thought wir mad. No mad fir a laugh, naw, these dudes wir mad fir doin real mad stuff. A dunno, happy slappin folk. But much worse. Much worse. Slashin an all that gang stuff. Anyway, the mad squad wir the important ones tae watch oot fir, coz they would hiv nae qualms aboot chibbin an English dude. A wrang word or lookin at somebody the wrang way wiz all it took. They needed nae excuse. Wee Sean actually told him tae keep his trap shut aroon the psychos just in case they took exception tae his accent. We'd've knocked any of them out if it came tae a square go, but it wiz nae worth it coz they'd just cut ye up when they got the chance, so it wiz always better to stay schtoom, don't face up to them. That wiz the mantra, man. An it wiz actually easy coz none of them wir in any ay oor classes. They wir in the remdems. Oh, it means remedial.

Some of them played in the fitball team as well, so we wir alright with them. After big Niall got injured we asked Clem tae be in the school team, but the guy had no interest in fitball. Strange, man, innit? He looked as if he could handle it though, but we foon oot he wiz intae rugby instead. My da always told me tae never trust someone who didnay like fitball. He had nae interest in it at all, don't git me wrang, it didn't make him a bad person or anythin like that. The guy wiz just different. For one, he didnay like any of the bands that we wir all intae. Well, loads really, but a suppose *The Killers, The Fratellis, The Kaiser Chiefs, 50 Cent, Kanye* an bands like that wiz what we banged oot. My da said that you can tell a lot about someone by the music they listened tae, so a asked him: 'Wit music are you intae, my man?' It wiz all these bands a'd never heard of an some other stuff that your granny would pure listen tae man. Each tae our own, eh? Aye, a suppose it wiz like all that stuff Rosie Farrell listened tae as well. A dunno wit it wiz, but it wiz pure mince. Whatever it wiz.

A didnay mind the guy. It wiznay like we wir goin tae be best buddies or anythin, but the impression a got wiz that there wiz somethin weird aboot him, an a'm no just sayin that coz it's easy tae say that now. If ye don't believe me, you can ask any of the boys a roll with. We all hid the same impression. A wiznay jealous coz Rosie fancied him, no way man. Loads of girls fancied him, that's the way of the world when a new guy or girl comes tae a new school. Unless they've been dookin for chips they'll attract some sort of attention; it's no big revelation man. A didnay sweat it. A think Liam wiz a wee bit jealous coz he'd snogged Rosie a couple of times, but he said she wiz way too oot there for him. Like in her heed. A bit of a looper. Naw, a don't mean she wiz like any of the mad squad looper. Looper in a good way.

A think it wiz actually *her* that told Liam tae sling *his* hook; the bold Liam told us that he didnay want anythin tae do with her because she wouldnay let him...erm...sleep with her. Aye right Liam! You cannay really blame her anyway. See all that terrible music an emo or goth look, a cannay be doin with all that. A mean she'd've been a pure stunner if she'd've scrubbed all that black shite aff her face an dressed properly an no like a pure tinker. But sayin that there wiz somethin cool aboot her as well. She wiz different. She didnay slap it on like the rest of the socks in our year. A liked Rosie, but a think she thought a wiz a bit of a nonce. Probably coz she hated fitball an me doin the boys thing. She wiz one of them men haters. A think a wiz the only one who wiznay surprised when Rosie an Clem got the gither. Actually, a wiznay surprised by anythin that happened. Especially in here. A said tae the lads, ages ago, that somethin like this wiz goin tae happen. You kin ask them if ye don't believe me. A'm just glad we nivir really let Clem roll wey us, you nivir know how it couldiv ended up fir us.

Aye, a do think Cora wiz put out by it all. Well it meant that her best pal wiz no aroon as much as she wanted.

Resentful? Aye, that's the word.

She wiz awright, wiz Cora, but a nivir fancied her or anythin like that. The lads used tae call her a pure mad stalker burd. She used tae have a thing for me, but a wiznay intae her at all. She wiz alright lookin, a mean she wiznay a dog or anythin, but she had a wee bit of a reputation aroon the school. The wee second- an third-years used tae shout, 'Cora Kelly, could gobble a welly.' But, if you believed all the stories you'd think Cora wiz out...erm...sleepin wey a different dude ivry night ay the week. Actually a know of one guy thit shag...erm...slept wey her coz he wiz shoutin his mouth aff aboot it. He plays for my fitball team. Naw, he's no a mate of mine, he's a bit ay a pleb if truth be told. Naw, it's a team ootside school. He's at college or uni or somethin. He hid no idea that a knew Cora. Anyway, that put me well aff her. Naw, she's alright is Cora, a good laugh at times, but there's no way a'd ivir go there. No way.

A'm glad a kept my distance fae that lot.

Yiv no idea how glad a am.

Mr Goldsmith's Astonishment

It's all extremely bewildering, how does one comprehend such a thing? As a schoolteacher it is one of your worst nightmares. It's the utter waste of it all that saddens me terribly. In our position sometimes we have the ability to foresee things, hypothesise and make accurate predictions about our students. But this! This is something that happens elsewhere. I had absolutely no idea at all, no inclination. Even if I delve into the deep recesses of my own mind, which I have subsequently done, there is no intimation, no caveat, no clue that I could pinpoint or signify. Nothing. If anything it makes one question the validity of one's profession, and just how qualified one is within it. I can tell you I have questioned myself many times over this issue. I am astounded by it all, if truth be told.

I recognised that Clem wasn't altogether charmed by the idea of heading up north. Well, who would at such a tender age? Leaving behind all his friends, his school and, in actuality, his culture. It would take a much determined and strong willed young person to cope with such a drastic alteration in life. Don't get me wrong it wasn't as though he was dreading the prospect either. I found him to be a young chap full of wanderlust and inquisitiveness. I can recall a conversation we had about the impending scene in which I openly encouraged him to approach his new life in Glasgow as a kind of anthropological adventure. I strived to remove any notion of trepidation he had in his mind. I saw this counselling, if you would like to refer to it as such, as an integral part of my position. I suppose in many ways I failed in that respect. I have subsequently cursed my prognosis.

Oh, yes, yes. A model student. A model student. He, along with a great many of my students, had an impressive appetite for knowledge. He devoured books, all kinds of literature. Like many boys of that age, he had a considerable zest for the work of the beat poets, however he wasn't limited to that. He approached their work with a great deal of fervour. What was impressive was that he didn't make the mistake that many others have made over the years, in that he didn't eulogise over the poems and/or the poets. He respected the writing, certainly, but he was also astute enough to distance himself from the work with a critical eye. He could effectively articulate why he liked a certain book or poem and, conversely, why he didn't.

Oh, my apologies. Unfortunately pounding the desk is an insufferable habit I have picked up over the years. It generated enormous hilarity in many of my classes. How can I hope to instil passion in my students if I myself have none? For my wife's sake, I am happy to report this habit doesn't extend to the family abode. Passion is important. Yet, there is a marked distinction between passion and, well, passion. A notable dichotomy. Excuse my floundering.

He was a joy to teach. A joy. An energetic participant in class, always active, always consistent in his comportment.

It's all unfathomable, isn't it?

In trying to account for a significant raison d'être I can only assume that, perhaps, too many of my lessons were rather too male orientated, aggressive and testosterone filled. I am referring to the writers and the literature studied. I have therefore posed the question to myself: were we, I, sub-consciously objectifying the female and, in doing so, heightening masculine prowess and control? If that is the case then I fully acknowledge and accept responsibility. Mea Culpa as they say. Furthermore, on a more philosophical level, is one inherently bad or is it merely a question of nature or nurture? It certainly is food for thought I should think. What is to become of our education structures? Of our professional integrity? Obviously, I have no expertise on the education system in Scotland, but I am still puzzled how this could have happened. In fact more astonished and saddened than puzzled. It's the waste of future hopes and aspirations. Saddened indeed.

Mr Cunningham's Mistrust

Listen, I'm not a fool. I can probably tell you what Pauline Croal said. Obviously not verbatim but I'd wager I'd get close to the gist of it; that we were all a shower of unfriendly dullards, set in our ways, devoid of any enthusiasm with regards to our profession. As Head of English at the school for years, I've heard this many times. I'd like to see the state of her after five, or so, years in this job.

Christ, these new teachers make me laugh, they waltz in here with their glistening teaching diplomas still warm in their pockets, revolutionary methods and heads full of ideology, then one of the first things they do is start shouting their mouths off, barking complaints at anyone unfortunate enough to be in close proximity, they have the temerity to point the finger at seasoned and experienced professionals; teachers, valued colleagues, who have had to wade through the turbulent seventies and eighties and emerged on the other side somewhat tarnished but gifted individuals nevertheless. Okay, so some of them are embittered and threadbare, but they are entitled to be after years of strife, are they not? It's hardly their fault now, is it? Don't expect me to sit here and perform some sort of self-flagellation because it won't happen.

Oh God no, I'm not suggesting that's any excuse for what happened.

Pauline Croal was a hard worker. She had good classroom management skills, which is probably the biggest worry when the new intake come swanning in. In that regard I had no concerns at all, absolutely none. As head of department probationers can be a headache at times, but she coped admirably from day one. I never heard any negative feedback from the students. Similarly I never heard any positive ones either. She was a capable teacher, that was evident. Personally I found her a touch snooty and aloof.

Undoubtedly, I thought that she was a good-looking young woman, I think most of the male staff, and the male student body, did also. Nevertheless I don't appreciate the insinuation. I'm a married man. Happily. One thing experience has taught me in this job is to be a good judge of character and I can tell you one thing, I didn't trust her. It was as simple as that. I didn't give her a hard time or anything, she got treated like any other member of staff but, the fact remains, I didn't trust the woman. As I said, I'm a good judge of character. With this incident the paradox is, on one hand, I was pretty much spot-on while, on the other, I was way off the mark. That I'm well aware of. No, I don't think there was anything I could have done. Even those with the foresight and inside knowledge couldn't have had an impact. There was no indication whatsoever. You just don't expect the unexpected. We're teachers, not detectives, psychologists or mind-readers. You can't apportion blame with this, myself and my colleagues are absolved from any finger wagging.

Rosie Farrell's Mum's First Impression

Well I have to say I was getting worried about our Rosie. She was dressing like one of them depressed lassies you see in the centre of town. You know, the ones who loiter behind the bookshop in Buchanan Street. I don't know what they do, they talk about music and watch the young lads play on the skateboards. And have their tights all ripped to shreds. Is *that* fashion? To me they all look the same, all dressed in black. And that make-up they all wear! What they need is a good wash, so they do. Anyway, I didn't want our Rosie to follow suit. It's not any parent's dream, is it? But I'd have rather her run around with that crowd than have her knocking about with a group of NEDs.

It's terrifying being a parent nowadays. You're scared stiff to let them out of your sight, then there's the whole teenage rebellion thing, not to mention the periods and growing up. As a mother you want to be pals with your daughter, good pals, you know, talking about girlie stuff and all that, but Rosie was no into all that, she hated all that pink girlie stuff, she even hated me washing her underwear. Well, she hated it being on show…like when it was drying. She washed it all herself and dried it in her room, which was an out of bounds area in our house. I don't think she was embarrassed about her body, I suppose she was just like any other sixteen-year-old girl in that respect. But we never spoke about things like that. We knew our boundaries. And I'm no stupid I knew she'd relax her rebellious streak. Sure, I was just the same when I was that age. My parents couldn't relate to me when I was sixteen, but now we're best friends and me and my mum tell each other everything, and I mean everything.

I was into *T.Rex* and *Bowie* and they couldn't understand why I dressed in platforms and had a face like an exploding rainbow. It's no different with Rosie, she's into all that miserable music, which I think is pure and utter rubbish. But I tell you something, you hear all these stories, don't you? Well, about how teenagers get obsessive about the music they're listening to and they carry out instructions they hear in the music. Look what happened in that school in America. Terrible that was. That was all to do with the music they were listening to, was it not? Anyway I was terrified that Rosie was becoming too dependent on that type of music. Not terrified as such, more concerned. She was becoming more withdrawn.

Rosie's dad is not on the scene. He used to say that it would have been better if we had had a wee boy instead of a girl because with a boy you only have one penis to worry about. Oh yes, that was a concern. A big concern. Every mother worries about that, don't they? I used to play the scene over and over in my head. I know my religion tells me that you can't abort, but, if I'm honest, if Rosie came in at that age and told me she was pregnant I'd march her down to the nearest clinic, I'm telling you I would. It'd just waste her life. You see all the young lassies around here pushing their buggies up and down with nowhere to go. The poor souls haven't a clue about how to take care of themselves never mind a bloody wean. She doesn't see her dad anymore. She used to, but no anymore. It's mostly his decision. It's not a major problem.

Rosie and Cora had been pals since primary school. I liked

wee Cora, but she was worrying me of late I have to say. In this place you can't go to Tesco but everyone knows what you had for your dinner, and wee Cora had started to get herself that bad reputation that no lassie wants. Well, it's plain to see, isn't it? That she was putting it about a bit. And that's up to her, as long as she's being careful, but in my mind I was wondering what our Rosie was up to while Cora was gaining that reputation. Was she just standing around a corner waiting for her? Or was she with the guy's pal? I tell you, my nerves were shattered. Don't get me wrong I don't expect her to be a saint or anything like that. Sure, I did the same when I was that age, well, just kissing and the like. What I'm saying is that, like any teenage girl, I was into boys and relationships, and first loves and going to the pictures and the discos. It was normal. But now it's all about sex, sex and more sex. I blame that bloody internet. Another worry was that in our day there were few cases of disease. Nowadays loads of girls have got something wrong with them, haven't they? I don't know. Well Chlamydia is the main one these days, isn't it? In my day we didn't even know there was something called Chlamydia. I was just waiting for the day when Rosie came in and told me that Cora was pregnant. I wouldn't have been that bit surprised one iota.

It wasn't as though I was over the moon, or anything like that, when Rosie brought Clem home for the first time. Obviously I noticed his strange name and his posh accent. But he was a nice laddie. You get that instinct about things. My first impression of him was that he was well mannered and charming. I could see why Rosie had gone for someone like him. You see, our Rosie has always thought most of the guys at her school were stupid, whereas Clem was the opposite. I'll tell you what was more important to me: Rosie seemed to be a lot happier after she met Clem. They became inseparable pretty quickly. He was always around at the house, always polite and friendly. I also noticed that she started listening to different music... Well, for example, I could hear her in her bedroom listening to *The Smiths,* who I remember from before I even had Rosie. I didn't much care for them then; all that dancing with flowers and old men's specs wasn't for me, thank you very much. It was all the weird people who were into them. But it was a welcome departure from that other garbage Rosie listened to. Our own relationship grew stronger too, I think. We would talk more about things, not their relationship of course, but maybe what they'd seen at the pictures, or she'd tell me about a gig they had been to. We communicated better, but I was always aware not to probe too much or those bridges would have been destroyed.

There was nothing to suspect. On the surface it appeared to be like any other teenage relationship. Normal. It starts off as a form of infatuation but we all know how quickly that can change and, before you know it, your world has caved in. There was no change with them two. They were good together. They were a good couple. The one concern I had about the relationship was that Clem told me he was returning to England when he finished school. I don't know where exactly. Where was he from again? Eastbourne? Well, I presumed that's where he was heading back to, then.

Naturally I didn't want our Rosie to go to England, so a part of me was hoping that the relationship would collapse. Selfish I know. But it's just the two of us. Always has been really. There has been no one else since Rosie's dad. Regardless of what I felt, or what I secretly wished for, I didn't want it to collapse quite in the way it did. No way did I expect that. No mother would want that. No person would want that. With what's happened now I wish her going to England was the only concern I had.

I always regarded myself to being a good judge of character, how wrong was I?

Pauline Croal's First Impression of Clem

Clem was a welcome addition to my class because he was, first and foremost, interested in the subject and showed a keenness and thirst for knowledge. He was obviously well schooled down south. He had picked up some good habits. I think he was somewhat frustrated at the level of his peers. Perhaps not the level as such, but certainly the apathy that surrounded him. Before Clem entered the class, discussion and debate was practically non-existent. It was reduced to a case of 'what does this mean, Miss?' and 'why is he saying this, Miss?' Not very adventurous, I'm afraid. Clem's level of enquiry was far and away more advanced than anyone else in that class. I liked having him there.

Yes, I suppose he did become one of my favourite students.

Any teacher who tells you that they don't have a favourite student is lying; usually it's a student who is an academic high achiever and one who gives them no behavioural problems. In my experience certain people equate good discipline with good teaching methods. Of course, it's related, but we can all scare a first-year class into submission and then not teach them anything. That's what a lot of teachers do, I have to say. The trouble is, they believe themselves to be good teachers. However, in my opinion they are nothing short of lazy teachers. They fear change, being knocked off their pedestal, or having their knowledge put into question. Or doubt.

In a sense I could relate to some of the students better than I could some of my colleagues. One reason would be down to the age gap. I was closer in age to the students than I was with the vast majority of my peers. I like teenagers. Well, mainly because they have a vibrancy and vivacity that rubs off on me. Maybe I involuntarily missed my teen years. No, I didn't hanker for them. I had no designs to return to those days. None whatsoever. What I am trying to say is that I think teachers should actually like teenagers; they should enjoy the company of teenagers, should they not? I don't see any transgression in this, or any conflict with my profession. Naïve maybe, but it's my belief.

Is that my charge?

It wasn't a question of attraction; it's not as simplistic as that. As a human being I could understand why he would have been regarded as attractive, why many of the girls found him fetching. Yes, of course, I thought he was handsome. That's not a crime, is it? I didn't for one moment think to myself, how lovely his eyes were, for example, or anything else for that matter. Yes, there were a few comments by female staff members, but nothing that could be construed as sinister or underhand. They were more like complimentary and gracious observations really.

He was the kind of student I took up teaching for. The one who keeps you on your toes; the one who delves below the surface of literature, trying to grind it down and deconstruct it by any means possible. Getting their teeth into it, in a snarling way. Gnawing away at it until it concedes defeat. I had always viewed it as a game, a competition, between the books and myself, a competition in which I was always victorious. We shared a commonality in our analytical approach of the subject. Of course, I am speaking about a sixteen-year-old's approach here; I know that, most definitely, mine was much more refined. Let's just say that we were on the same wavelength.

No teacher sets out to get close to his or her students in that way. These things tend to evolve from areas such as respect and reverence. Clem was intent on gaining an A' pass in his end-of-year exam and I was going to try and facilitate this. I told him if he was willing to put the work in, then I would help him. Yes, that meant outside the classroom environment, but within the boundaries of the school building itself. Let's see, there were the homework clubs, special study groups, late night library opening...all these things were school initiatives. I was just one of many teachers who gave their time to assist. Yes, we were paid. Clem used to come to the Tuesday and Thursday special study group. They could take various forms, from the student doing their own homework, collaborating with other students on a task...like essay writing and structure, for example. Sometimes it could take the format of a teacher led discussion or lecture. The numbers fluctuated, sometimes as much as fifteen other times as low as two.

Rosie Farrell never came along. Clem always did, alone. I was impressed with his drive. He was a determined young man and I had no doubts in my mind that he would gain his A' pass. He told me he was eager to return to the south, I don't think he was enjoying his experience in Glasgow. That's an understatement really, given what we now know. I did have sympathy with him as this place can be pretty unforgiving, especially if you come from the wrong side of the tracks. It wasn't necessarily an anti-English sentiment he was fighting, it was the desire to improve his standing; he was also a victim of his class status. He was from a middle-class background, that was apparent, and he was battling against that. I could empathise with him there. I thought he appreciated my understanding. I offered support one specific time, but only because he had been injured. Nothing too serious, just some bruising around the eye. But it was plain to see that the psychological damage was much more profound. I bumped into him in the corridor one morning. He appeared troubled, frustrated and upset. As I said, I offered support and, perhaps inadvertently, a hand of comfort. It wasn't anything that could have been misinterpreted. Naturally I felt sorry for him, he was my student. I liked having him in my class and he was in a bad place, a vulnerable place. All I wanted to do was help him. He declined. At the time I didn't know who did it, however I did have my suspicions. And in light of events, these suspicions proved to be pretty accurate.

Sometimes we spoke about potential universities and courses. Literature was his course of choice. Yes, I think he did value my opinion.

Well, it's not as though I walked about the school with my eyes and ears closed. I had heard and seen things. It was no secret that he and Rosie were an item. I felt neither injury nor delight. It was a perfectly natural occurrence.

Support? I neither supported nor condemned it. It wasn't my place. I have absolutely no idea why Rosie disliked me. Really, I don't consider my looks to be the catalyst for her abhorrence of me. Clem didn't have a crush on me! He was far too astute, and mature, for all that nonsense. Rosie had nothing to be jealous about. If I was a threat to her then it was all in her adolescent imagination.

Rosie Farrell's Love of Games

My mum was dead protective. She was mad scared that I was going to get up the duff or something. She kept going on about Cora and how she was doing herself no favours and all that. I didn't have a clue what she was going on about half the time. She used to turn into a pure psycho mum sometimes. Burst your arse so it did. But she was alright with Clem. She didn't mind him coming round the house so often, we'd just go to the room and listen to music…I don't know all sorts. *The Shins, Gorky's Zygotic Mynci*, he liked them, *Clap Your Hands Say Yeah, Belle and Sebastian* I liked them. Loads of stuff. He said he was going to teach me the guitar. Be waiting for a long time for that one.

We'd talk about stuff and do other stuff…you know, other stuff.

No way, I've got my head screwed on. I knew what I was doing. I'd like to think we influenced each other. I'm not a pure mad dafty spa who just sat there and swooned over him. That's not my bag. I'll leave all that carry on to the wee lassies with hula-hoop heads. I've got a Scooby. Scooby Doo…Clue. Well, I'm clued in. Just coz he knew all these big fancy dan words and had a posh accent didn't make him the brain of Britain. He could be thicko of the week as well, you know.

We just started talking about music and gigs we'd been to and things like that. It was alright. He was sound. Then after he stopped all that *emo-chick* crap we got on like Ken and Barbie. Well, the main reason he was different from the other guys was coz he was clever, we'd all pure look at each other in class when he spoke, in that what-the-fish-is-he-talking-about? look. We really didn't know what he was gibbering on about most of the time. And that was in all the classes. He was way above us. In schoolwork, I mean. He told me his last school was totally different, everybody like did their work, studied hard and didn't mess about in class. Sounds a hoot! But I liked listening to him prattle on and on about stuff that I didn't need to know. When he was shouting it off in class I was like dead chuffed that he was my type of bf. Maybe you could call it pride, but I don't think it was. Some of the teachers didn't have a Scooby what he was on about half the time. He showed the teachers up so he did. I also felt sorry for him a wee bit as well because he had no pals up here. Some of the sixth-year guys started chatting to him, but I could tell they thought he was a bit of a zoomer. I saw one of them on MSN slagging him off. The funny thing was the guy who was doing it is a right space cadet. The guys don't generally do irony in here. But it wasn't out of any sympathy that we started spending time with each other. I did sort of fancy Clem. We just sort of clicked and the rest fell into place.

We'd chat about tonnes of stuff. Mad stuff. Like if someone was playing you in a film, who would it be? The person had to look a wee bit like you and have a similar attitude, so there would be no Jude Laws or Angelinas. I picked that guy from *Brick* for Clem. On that day I remember talking about band names on our way to school. It was freezing. Both of us made breath circles from the cool air. Mine were bigger and better. His were wee baby ones. I think he let anxiety get in the way of a good breath circle. I started talking about the most crappy things imaginable. Pure red neck stuff. But that was me, I suppose.

'What would you call your band if you were in one?' I asked him.

'I don't know.' At that stage I was thinking, where's your spontaneity man?

'Don't talk rubbish. You do. Everyone has played that game, come on, what is it?' I could see his thought processes at work. I liked it when I could see him think. You know, deeply. But this time he was thinking about something else. We know what that was now. But I could tell at the time. I should be a blinking psychologist or psychiatrist or something like that. I didn't know the difference actually. I bet Clem would have.

'It's *Approaches to Learning*,' he said. I puffed my cheeks out and made this raspberry noise.

'That's pure mince.'

'You think?'

'A hundred percent.'

'Okay, smart arse, what's yours?' he said.

'Don't know, never really thought about it.' I was taking the piss, wasn't I? Cora's band name was *Aloud Pussycat*. She was trying to mix *Girls Aloud* and *Pussycat Dolls*, both of whom are rank rotten and their severe names go hand in hand with their severe songs. Saying that, both names were much better than *Aloud Pussycat*. Conor's was *The Last of the Happymen*. Enough said. I liked the band name game it was a good way to pass the time. An even better way to break long silences. I did have some of them with Clem as well.

'Don't talk crap, come on I told you mine.'

'Okay, don't laugh?'

'Cross my heart.'

'Okay,' I said, 'it's *Bedroom Busker*.' Inspired or what? At one stage I was going to buy a bass guitar, start a band and call it *Bedroom Busker*. Obviously. I even went as far as going into the shop and trying one out, but I didn't have a Scooby what to do with it and the strings, I mean have you seen the size of those? They were like a baby's arm, you'd need fingers like courgettes to play them. But the bass was what I wanted. All female bass players are cool as. Like Kim Deal from *The Pixes* and David Bowie's bass player with the big afro. She's dead cool. And Mo Tucker from *The Velvet Underground*, even though she's a drummer, but it's the same thing really. I could just see myself plucking away with *Bedroom Busker*. Or should it be *The Bedroom Busker*? Decisions. Decisions.

'Utter utter crap,' Clem said.

'What?'

'I'd never buy anything from a band with a name like that.'

'You haven't a clue.'

Then there was this pure dead silence; Clem's head was obviously in the horrors. He was rubbing his hands as if washing them, transferring sweat from one to the other. There was no way I was grabbing that, even if he did offer me it. All clammy and minging hand. No chance. I think he was psyching himself up for the big faceoff. The funny thing was I was totally calm on that trip to school. That's ignorance for you.

He picked Ellen Page for me. I was like, 'who the hell's Ellen Page?' I hadn't seen *Juno* at that stage. I was secretly hoping he was going to say Winona Ryder or Zooey Deschanel, but I was actually really glad that it wasn't someone pure pot ugly.

Mr Goldsmith's Opinion

It's difficult to form an accurate opinion when one's only reference point is a fifteen-minute parents' evening twice a year. Nevertheless, one can draw particular conclusions and assumptions through their progeny. Mr and Mrs Curran were an impressive couple, Clem was their only child and they evidently transferred this impressiveness onto Clem himself. With some parents it can be an exhausting struggle of wills regarding their offspring's education, many parents, you see, believe that they could do a superior job, or, at very least, a more productive one themselves. One conducive to their child's specific requirements, I suspect.

We are all specialists it would appear. The Currans were different in this regard; they were hugely supportive of the school and the tactics implemented by the staff here. They certainly did not possess the socially accepted and ubiquitous *I could do better than that* attitude that some of our parents shared. That is not to say they passively accepted the school's stance on Clem's education without enquiry either. They would ask pertinent questions and make regular enquiries regarding the advancement of their son's education. During our brief discussions they intimated that they wanted Clem to study law or medicine. One of the elite professions. Don't get me wrong, they were not elitist themselves. Like most parents they simply wanted the best for their child. Nonetheless I knew, from conversations I'd had with the boy himself, that he had no inclination or leaning for this area of study. I would go as far as to suggest that the sheer notion of studying law or medicine was abhorrent to the boy. Oh, no, no, no, I was in no

41

position to dissuade the desire and wishes of his parents. As a teacher the powers I had in my possession would only allow me to put it to parents that their son or daughter was showing signs of encouragement in a specific field, and that it could be that he or she may wish to continue with their development in said field, but to disagree and discourage the will of the mother and father, well, that was not part of the remit of a school teacher. Also, these powers I talk of are docile at best. You have to remember we are dealing with adolescents here and teachers should not allow these sensitivities to vanish within the context of the classroom. It is also worth remembering that on the surface students can appear to be full of wisdom and maturity, however one has to consider that they are still very much at the emotionally pre-pubescent stage. Perchance it would go a long way in explaining this ghastly episode.

I am afraid we did not actually operate on a personal level. We kept our meetings cordial but businesslike. To my knowledge they had a good standing in the community and were well liked. They weren't philanthropic or anything of that nature, my belief is that they were charitable with their time. My opinion of them was that they were decent, honest folk.

I think it is practically impossible to evade gossip mongering after the event. On the other hand, it is natural to speculate and feast on a diet of conjecture when something like this occurs. What I do not concur with is fabrication and untruths. For my own part I have taken a vow of silence in the sense that I refuse to participate in the idle tittle-tattle that tends to encase these things. The facts must surface before the indulgence of fiction and supposition.

Clem informed us, his teachers, after only the first week of the summer term, that he was leaving. I agree it was rather an abrupt end to his school career with us. When he enlightened us to the fact that he was heading for Glasgow, well, it did strike me as somewhat incongruous. This was a vital year for him, in terms of exam success, future considerations and employment prospects and given the value that his parents placed on his education here, I found it odd that they were willing to fracture the continuity of it all. To be perfectly honest with you I thought that something untoward was afoot. No, I did not share that view with any of my colleagues. I carried out my professional duty and supported Clem in any way possible, especially in a time that could have been perceived as transitionally turbulent. I offered my services to him if he had any academic queries or concerns. In this modern technological age it is not too difficult to track one down, is it? Within the legal parameters that is. It is not the job of the school to question parents in these matters. It was presumed, and correctly so, that Mr Curran had either taken up a position in Scotland with a new company, or had been offered a transfer with his existing one. These are precarious times, gone are the days when the workforce can pick and choose. Our politicians and bankers have seen to that. Clem was simply an additional victim of the credit crunch. There are many victims in all this, are there not? Least of all the boy himself. That's the waste. The destruction of young lives. With this in mind, blame doesn't come into it for me at this moment. In many ways we are all to blame.

Cora Kelly's Isolation

I had a pure red neck for Miss Croal by the way. Everyone was talking about how she only took that swotty nerd group coz Clem was going to it. Some wee guy in third-year said that she gave him…well, you know…under the desk, but you can take that with a pinch of salt. Or a sack of salt if it came from the third-years. They're just full of wee numpties who talk mince all the time. I know. I felt a bit sorry for Rosie coz folk were saying that Croal fancied her bf. See, I thought she did at the beginning, right? But after a few months I could tell that she just liked him coz he was the brainiest in the class and she thought all the rest of us were pure thickos. She used to stand there and say in that posh West End voice of hers:

'I can't believe how limited a vocabulary you have, Cora Kelly.'

'Aye right ye are, Miss, nae hassle,' I'd say.

She was a bit round the twist. I think that's why Rosie hated her. I dunno. What's the difference between hate and dislike. Anyway, she didn't like her, case closed. Loads of pupils hated certain teachers. It's not a sin. She used to go berserk if you had your moby out, or if it went off in your bag or you got caught sending a text message. I got nabbed in loads of classes. Got loads of punnies for an all. Nightmare.

Erm…Punishment exercises, punny for short.

I couldn't be bothered with her, she was too posh for me, and I hated the way she wore tight clothes to impress the guys. All boobs and smiles. I could just imagine her when she was at school herself. Miss Prim n Proper. I bet she was like one of the lassies off of the *The Sound Of Music*. Then she comes in here and thinks she's down with what goes on in this area. "I'm a homegirl like you lot. I understand your plight." No way, man; she's no getting away with that.

Of course I was happy for Rosie. I knew from day one that she fancied Clem so I was down with it when she started going out with him. He was alright. I quite liked him, but after speaking to him I knew that I'd never fancy him. Too swotty for my liking. Anyway I didn't have a Scooby what he was going on about half the time. The important thing was that she liked him and he liked her. Well that happens when your pal gets a bf. What did you want me to do? Pure stand about like a gooseberry? It's not as if I was, like, pure wandering the streets on my own. Who do you think I am, *Mrs Bean* or something? I was seeing this guy anyway. He's no from this school, he's at college or uni or something. Conor Duffy was hanging around like a baby's nappy as well. But he soon got the bum's rush. He thought he could just snap his fingers and I'd come running like some wee lapdog. He thought he was pure God's gift…he was alright but I think he was raging a bit when Clem came coz Clem was better looking than him and all the attention moved from Conor to Clem.

That's none of anybody's business by the way. I don't see how that's got anything to do with anything. Everybody has always got an opinion about me and making up pure porkies, they should just ask me outright and I'll tell them straight… You can do anything you want, I'm still no telling you about any of that stuff. All this has got nothing to do with me by the way, so I can walk if I want.

They spent all the time with each other, even at lunchtime. Me and Rosie used to go up to the chippy at lunchtime, buy a roll n chips, smoke a fag, drink a can of *Irn Bru*. Everyday without fail, even when it was pure lashing down. Then Clem came on the scene and all of a sudden she was into going to that salad place down the precinct instead. It was up to her if she wanted to eat that Hollywood size-zero scran, it's not as if I was going to fall out with her coz of it. What was I going to do about it? You just have to accept that that's part of life. She was in mad love. So was he. At least, I think he was. If he wasn't he was a brilliant liar then, wasn't he? And the thing is all this stuff makes me think that's exactly what he was, a brilliant liar. Rosie was my friend for yonks and I can't remember one lie she told me.

Confide? What does that mean? Aye, me and Rosie used to talk about everything. I'd tell her all my news and she'd tell me all hers. No, I didn't tell her all the details, some things you don't need to know, right? Aye, I'm sure she did the same. But that's not lying, is it? They are totally different. I asked her if she loved Clem and she told me all this guff about love being hard to define and that it was too abstract to even try to understand it. I had to ask her what abstract meant. Anyway the fact is she was talking utter mince. So I asked her again, 'do you love him, or not?' Then she said that she did. When I asked her if Clem loved her she prattled on about love being abstract again, but eventually she said that, even though he hadn't said it to her face, she thought that he did. If that was good enough for Rosie…it was good enough for me too. Rosie had her head screwed on about all that stuff. I mean you should hear some of the girls in our year talking about how they're pure in love with some guys after just one snog. They haven't a Scooby what love's all about. I'm not saying I do either, but I don't go about saying, 'oh, I'm pure in love with so and so' or 'I pure love so and so to death' after one conversation on Bebo.

Friends stick together, don't they? I knew that he was going to go back down to where he was from after his exams. Rosie told me he wanted to go to some uni down there, in some place I'd never heard of. I'm not great with my geography. I didn't know what he wanted to study, probably law or doctoring. I knew that when he went back down south that's when Rosie would need me around again, wouldn't it? That's when she'd need me more. And I'd be there for her coz that's what friends are for. I'd be there for her always.

When they were together it's not as if she pure blanked me or anything, it's just that I didn't see her as much as I used to. Only at school and the odd time when she stayed back to do some extra art. We still had a howl though. I'd no idea that she was thinking of going to England to study. She didn't tell me that. I always thought that she wanted to go to uni up here and study art or design, or something creative like that. That's what she told me anyway. But she didn't tell me that she'd applied to some uni down there. Where was it again? That's right, Brighton. Sounds alright actually. Couldn't be doing with that accent though. Can't for the life of me understand why anyone would want to be around that twenty-four seven. Do your absolute nut in, so it would. The funny thing is, see if it was a guy at our school, you know, just one of the normal guys, Conor's mates or something, there's no way in hell she would have followed him around the country. No way. What's that word when you're mad for someone and you can't let them out of your sight? Infatuate, that's it. She was infatuate with him. She'd have done anything for him. Well, she did. But I'm no that stupid, there's no chance that I'd be running around after some pure mad guy like a wee lapdog just because he was, like, dead cool and mad different from the rest of the guys. Life's too short for all that. And, anyway, it's much better if they're doing all the running than that oh-I'm-so-in-love-I-want-to-die crap.

Mr Cunningham's Inclination

No teacher in their right mind wants to remain after the bell, unless they have no option. Parents' night, for example. What I'm talking about is the extra-curricular activities, or other altruistic things teachers get themselves involved in. I've said it time and time again, they get no reward, financially or otherwise, for the work they do. Yes, periodically I have questioned the motives of certain members of staff. Having said that, it's vital in any school environment that they have things like a football team, music clubs and drama clubs to participate in. Sometimes the school environment is the only solace these kids get. I ran a creative-writing class years ago, or tried to. It's a thankless task. In this job you're constantly being let down by students. In my experience, you'll be disappointed somewhere down the line.

When the possibility of special study evenings was first muted there weren't many teachers queuing up to put themselves forward, even though it was paid work. A pittance for what they expected of you to be honest: stay behind on a Tuesday and Thursday night. Babysitting. Naturally it was hard to fill the position. Yes, it was down to me to help fill the study evenings. It's not something I would normally ask a probationer teacher to do; well, for one, they don't have the experience, and two, they have enough on their plate trying to settle into a new profession, a demanding profession. I didn't ask them for those reasons alone. Pauline Croal approached *me* with the suggestion herself. I consulted a colleague and it was agreed that we would give her the responsibility of running the evening classes. They weren't compulsory classes for the students, so in that sense the heat was off. Nevertheless, it did demonstrate her eagerness to assimilate with the students and the demands of the job. You have to be careful of an over abundance of enthusiasm, it can be misplaced and misconstrued, especially by colleagues. Teachers can be a sensitive breed; they don't like being down the pecking order when it comes to popularity, so while you can be extremely popular with the students, you can find yourself ostracised in the staff room. It's a balancing act. My initial worry concerning Pauline Croal was that she would find herself isolated very quickly, if she didn't change her ways a bit. By that I mean she'd have to try and curb her eagerness to please and be accepted; also, and this is a prickly subject, I thought she'd have to alter the way she dressed somewhat. It was a touch suggestive, but more than that, it was inappropriate for a school environment. The way she dressed, in my view, was a major misjudgement on her part and misread the male, and female, students' mentality. She was laying herself open to an enormous amount of criticism both inside and outside the classroom. I wouldn't say that I reluctantly agreed that she could oversee the evening classes, nevertheless I did accept her willingness to do it with some degree of caution.

It became apparent very quickly that something inappropriate was going on. In this job you learn to filter the yarns from the bona fide. Bad news, or in this case inflammatory news, can act as a fire's oxygen in a school. Tongues wagged. But I have seen events of this nature play themselves out before. This could have been the catalyst for the boy's problems with his peers. And, let's be honest, the subsequent event. As head of department, I had to approach the issue with prudence. It was no time for charging in like a gang of disgruntled NEDs. There were no facts on the table and without facts hearsay doesn't help us advance things. I had an inclination, but like everyone else I heard it through the students. Some sixth-year lads I taught, good lads. Interested in their football and music, not much energy saved for their schoolwork, I have to say, but trustworthy fellows. They weren't part of the NED culture in the school, which was a relief, so their inference had some weight and validity. Who better than sixth-year boys to know what the goings on in a school were...sixth-year girls, indeed. Quite right. Quite right.

No, I didn't investigate as such. How do you propose approaching such a thing? Instead I kept my eyes and ears open and endeavoured to observe Pauline Croal more closely. The lad in question I didn't teach, but I was aware that he was a gifted student. It's always difficult coming to a new school, but he had fitted in rather well by all accounts. Yes I was aware that he and Rosie Farrell were an item. I taught her in third- and fourth-year, a nice girl. Unusual, but nice. Her idiosyncrasies were certainly poles apart from her peers. I'd have never thought she'd have been implicated in this. By proxy or whatever. Never. My experience informs me that you can never be one hundred percent sure, can you?

Of course, we, as a school, have to hold our hands up and accept our share of responsibility. Perhaps some of the staff could have made more valued judgements and acted before the situation got out of hand, which quite clearly it did. Obviously I am talking about colleagues such as Pauline Croal here, who was close to the boy, if you believed the

51

school's rumour-mill. In this instance I hold my hands up and say that I did believe it initially. I am not saying that their dalliance had a direct effect in the event in question, but, I have to say, it could have been intrinsically linked in some perverse way. Everything has a cause and effect after all.

Conor Duffy's Brainwave

It wiz Cora who first attracted ma attention tae it. So did big Liam iz well, coz he wiz in her English class. The thing iz, big Liam wiznay the sharpest tool in the box so she wouldnay've givin him any attention at all. But big Liam said she used tae swoon over him in class. That's just him bein jealous a suppose. Then he told me that she wiz all over him in the swots class after school...his wee sister goes tae the class sometimes, and she said that she felt that she wiz intrudin on two people hivin a date. I wiz like that, get in there my son! Wit guy wouldnay've wanted tae sha...erm...kiss Miss Croal? Am tellin ye he wiz the talk ay the common room fur a while. Come tae think of it, he's still the talk ay the common room. Then wee Cora said that she suspected somethin and if it wiz true that she wiz goin tae scud him full force on the bawz... erm...penis... an then tell Rosie. An I thought she wouldiv as well.

Clem knew all the rumours iz well coz when any ay us tried tae ask him aboot it, he always said somethin we didnay understand an then storm aff. He got that mad look in his eye an you were like, nae danger man, A'm no goin there. Am no gettin involved in any that caper. A'll tell you wit though, if it wiz true he wiz some liar coz he an Rosie were still like Velcro knickers kickin aboot the school...aye she heard. She must've. You cannay keep anthin quiet at this school, we even know wit girls are...erm...on their period. Wit I meant iz that you cannay keep anythin a secret, the world is too small, man; walls have ears an all that. Rosie must've known. But the funny thing about it wiz that Cora didnay tell her, now that wiz dead weird coz if that'd been ma best mate I'd've told him there an then, but Cora said nothin. Maybe she knew somethin we didnay. Some folk still think Rosie got wind ay somethin coz she's no that stupid. Rosie Farrell may be loads of things but she's no thick. If she did, it just shows you how much she wiz intae yer man. Maybe he wiz threatenin her or somethin an that's why she didnay dae anythin. A dunno, it's pure mental man. A still cannay get ma heed roon it.

A just think he hated it here, that he hated all the teachers, apart fae Miss Croal, an all the students. The NEDs used tae give him a hard time aboot his accent, slaggin him all the time, doin bad impressions an all that. They slaughtered him aboot his clothes as well, which wiz a pure joke considerin they're all sittin there wey their Primark trackies an white trainers on. A actually thought Clem's clothes were cool as. He looked a wee bit like a singer, but no one who looks like they've been dragged through H an M. Cooler than that.

Anyway, it wiz a sin fur him coz you couldnay even say anythin back tae them in case he'd git leathered after school. A cannay blame him. That's why a thought he went tae those classes after school, tae get away fae the NEDs. It wiz a sin for him man, am tellin you. A felt dead sorry fur the guy, coz he wiznay that bad so a had a wee brainwave, a approached one of the NEDs who played in the football team an ask them tae lay aff a bit. Bad move, man. Bad move. A just said, give the guy a break, man. An he turned roon an said: 'A'll fuckin break yer jaw if you speak tae me like that again, ya cheeky cunt'. Aye, it wiz Fran McEvoy. A thought a wiz in for it; that the squad would be waitin after school. For about two weeks a wiz terrified of them. At the end of the day a had tae let

Clem fight his own battles on that front. Look after number one. But, dude, man, the guy wiz getting a hard time fae all angles, the Croal stuff an the NEDs. He wiz one brave boy though, no doubt about that. One brave mother. A'd defy anyone tae do nothin in that situation.

Sometimes a think that maybe the fellas an me could hiv done a wee bit more, you know, iz a support fur the guy. Bring him intae the clan. That we could've invited him oot with us sometime. Up the town. Gigs. Shoppin. But, at the end of the day, if it doesnay click, it doesnay click. It would'iv been like tryin tae fit a triangle intae a circle, or somethin like that.

Rosie Farrell's Mortification

I might be daft but I'm no stupid, or the other way around. Do you think for one minute that I walked around that place and never heard a thing? Of course I heard what everyone was saying. Even my best pal was saying it, well, she wasn't exactly saying it, but she was part of all the gossip groups. Oh, I know Cora she'd have been right in the middle of them all, stirring it up. Although she told me afterwards that she was trying to shut them up, I didn't know if I believed her. We just had one of those rubbish arguments that nobody wins. I was saying to her:

'Aye some pal you are, didn't even say a word.'

And she was like, 'what do you mean, never said a word' I was the one trying to make sure your name was kept out of it.'

'Aye right,' I said.

'Aye right,' she said.

'You should have told me,' I said.

'You should be thanking me I never,' she said.

'There's no way I'm pure thanking you,' I said.

'Aye right,' she said.

'Aye right,' I said. And it went on like this for ages and nobody won the argument. I won't bore you with the rest of it. At the end of the day I could see her point, you know, when I played all the events over in my head. I was raging though. But then when I played *that* in my head, you know, why I was raging, I think it wasn't Cora I was raging at. No, it wasn't Clem either. It was myself for not realising it. I sort of had an idea that something was going on, but I guess I blanked it out of my mind. Well, that's what people do when they don't want to admit the truth, isn't it? I read that somewhere in a book about psychology or psychiatry or something like that, it was psycho something. Anyway it said that by not engaging with true events, that's the book's words by the way, by not engaging with true events you are consciously blanking it out of the mind. But the thing is, the harder you try to blank it out the more it takes over the things you think about. It was weird because I kept thinking about it all the time. All the time. I couldn't concentrate in any of my classes. I couldn't even do my art. It was mad as, so it was.

Then I got dead para...paranoid...and thought the whole school was gawking at me when I walked down the corridor. Especially all those mongo NEDs. Cora kept saying, 'why don't you say something?' But I just couldn't. I thought that if I asked him he'd have dumped me then and there. I was sort of loved up with him at the time. I couldn't just pure ask him outright. I was terrified. But that all changed. Another part of me was like, you have to trust him if you're going to have any future together, you have to be able to trust each other. The thing is he gave me no reason to think that anything bad was going on, apart from the gossiping and sniggers. He was just the same, nothing changed in him. And when I think back and ask myself was there any sign of anything strange going on, you know, in his behaviour, I'd have to say no. It was the same Clem as ever, but it was like one of those things that hovers over you, you know, like a bubble or a cloud or something. I couldn't stop thinking about it.

Then I did something really bad. Not like *bad* bad, but bad enough to make me feel bad. I didn't cry over it or anything like that, I just had this thing saying something in my head, 'I can't believe you did that, Rosie; I can't believe you did that.' Anyway, I stayed back late in the art room to start off my portfolio, I was just doing some life sketching, bowls and cups and fruit and stuff like that. Easy stuff. But it was all one big pretence. I did sketch a wee bit and I did need to get the portfolio started but I could just as easily have done it at home, the thing was I didn't tell Clem that I was staying back. I knew his study class finished at a certain time, so I just waited till ten minutes before it was over and then I waited outside for him to come out. No, I wasn't waiting on him. I didn't want him to see me. We hadn't planned it. I was actually waiting across the road so that when he came out I was ready to nick down and hide behind a car. I was standing there shaking. I was pure morto that I was doing this. That's just not what I do. Well, obviously it is now. Anyway, the next thing I know I see Clem coming out of the school's main doors, only he's not alone. I thought 'you cheeky little...' In front of the school as well. By this time I was in bits. I was livid. I was half going to run up to them and have it out right there and then. Thank God I didn't. But I could feel my anger getting the better of me, my hands were sweating and I was clenching them into a fist. The funny thing was though, there was this wee voice in my head saying, 'what are you doing, Rosie? You're making a complete fool of yourself. If he catches you it's curtains.' So I'm hiding behind this car and the next thing I know they're walking in my direction and I'm like, 'oh shite, oh shite,' then I realise that I'm right in the middle of a street where some of the teachers park their cars. They're that close that I can hear them talking. Clem's asking how many quotes he should be putting into his essay. I mean for God's sake! By this time I'm shifting around the parked car in case they see me. But they don't. It's the next car down they're standing at. Then something weird happened, they didn't say anything at all. They just stood there and said nothing, which seemed to go on for ages and ages. I was like, hurry up and go because my legs were killing me hunched there behind that car. But they said nothing until Croal broke the silence. She said, 'do you want a lift anywhere?' Then there was more silence until Clem broke it and said, 'no it's alright, I'm good thanks.' Or something like that. I was like, ah that's my boy. Then he went home and she drove away in her car...no, I can't remember what kind; I'm no really up with my car models. When I got home I had a pure red neck for what I did. But, at the end of the day, it put all that shite in my head to bed for a bit. So even though it was bad, it was a good bad. If you know what I mean. It confirmed everything to me.

I felt great after that. It sort of brought us closer together in a strange way. I wanted to trust him, and I knew he trusted me. The rumours were still floating about but who cares, right? The thing is, I was wondering why nobody said anything to her, other teachers I mean. Or why she still came to school. Not that she shouldn't have been in school because she'd done nothing wrong; it's just that I couldn't stand all those folk sneering at me all the time. I'd be pure stressed out of my nut. I've got to hand it to her she had balls of steel to continue showing her face in that school...well, because everyone gets a hard time...well, not everyone, but you know what I mean. Then all that changed, didn't it?

Clem didn't say anything at first but I knew he was getting a hard time. It's nothing new, anyone who dares to be a wee bit different, who likes a certain type of music or who wears a certain style of clothes or has a different hairstyle than everyone else even, gets a hard time. You see, you're not allowed to be different from everyone else. You've all got to like the same things, do the same things, go to the same places, have the same opinions, have the same interests and have the same level of bitchiness. Schools are bizarre places because everyone is just a clone of everybody else. How depressing is that? It's not as if I go out my way to be different, that's just the way I am. In my mind I don't consider myself to be different, it probably looks that way because I'm not like any of them. Obsessed with things like...crap TV. Who cares who's in the final of *Strictly Come Dancing*? I mean, who gives a toss? Clem was totally different from everyone else, and I'm not just talking about his accent. He was way more intelligent also, which never goes down too well. It wasn't really that much of a surprise that folk were slagging him all the time. Yes, it was mostly guys. I suppose it began with all the sixth-years, Conor Duffy and his cronies. Or 'crew' as they liked to call themselves. Clowns. It was mostly taking the piss and trying to imitate his accent. Cora told me most of what was going on. It wasn't like vindictive stuff or anything like that it was more immature wee boys talking shite behind someone's back stuff. I'll tell you what though, they would never have said anything to his face because Clem could have taken them apart with his tongue. It was sharp. Razor sharp. No, he didn't feel threatened by them. They weren't dangerous or anything like that, they just thought they were great and ruled the school. They thought they were in that horrific American TV programme…that's it, *Beverly Hills 902*…whatever it is.

The NEDs were the ones who scared him the most. He didn't like walking past them in the corridor or being in the same class as any of them. I don't think he'd experienced anything like that at his last school. In fact I knew he hadn't, he didn't need to tell me. So when he came up here it must have been some eye-opener for him. I remember explaining to him what the word NED actually meant. He thought it was hilarious. He thought the way their wee neddy hats sat on the top of their heads, you know, pure pointing upwards, was dead sinister. In a pathetic way. It was all a joke at first but you just knew that they were waiting for an excuse to do something. To get him. Not that they needed excuses to do what they wanted to do right enough. I always told him to stay well clear of them. The trouble was, they knew he was new to the place, new to Glasgow, and he wouldn't have had any friends or anything like that to back him up. In their heads they thought they could do anything and there would be no comeback for them. That's their mentality. That's how brainless they were. The sad thing is they were right. Who was going to do something to challenge them? The school? The Police? No chance. It didn't seem to bother Clem at first. I think half the battle was that he didn't have a Scooby what they were saying most of the time. Normal folk are hard enough to understand for Clem but the NEDs have their own special way of talking, it's like listening to pure thick people talking with a mouthful of lemons. Everything is said through the nose as if someone's constantly squeezing it for them. I haven't a clue what they are saying half the time. Then there's the sovvy rings that they all wear…sovereign rings; you buy them in town for dirt cheap. Pure tramps, man. The problem is they use the sovvy rings as knuckledusters as much as anything else. They used to walk about the school giving people dead arms, and you should see the bruise that it leaves. Can you imagine that on the face? But Clem thought the whole NED outfit was strange. He used to call it the NEDs' uniform. You should see them though, Glasgow's full of them. Like a plague. A cancer. Imagine if you were a tourist and you were faced with that?

Imagine if you had been Clem?

You could type NEDs into You Tube and you'd see them all dancing about, smoking joints and swigging Buckie in some park or in some pure dafty tink's house. They'd all have their arms around each other and, in most cases they'd be giving the finger. Or flashing their arses. Dead weird stuff. What do they call it? Homoerotic that's it. The worst was the music that accompanied their NED bonding; it was all that doof doof doof crap. The sort of music that would make you want to rip your ears out of your head. You Tube was full of clips with our school's NEDs. To be honest I don't think they were that into their music, they wouldn't have known a good record if it popped up in their curry and chips. What they knew about groups, bands, songs, albums and that, you could have written on the back of a stamp. That was another reason they gave Clem a hard time, they ripped him about him doing music at school. See in their mind that was only for the fags. God knows what they'd have made of Clem's taste in music.

Mr Goldsmith's Elucidation

It wasn't for me to judge why the family chose to live in Scotland. To my recollection they have no family connections to Glasgow. Actually, I am unsure if they have any family in the Eastbourne area. Glasgow, as I am led to believe, is culturally miles away from Eastbourne. Not that I have spent enough time there to make an accurate assessment. Yes, I would say that I was slightly concerned about Clem's moving. In the main, my concerns were about his education more than the lifestyle change; however, I understand that they are not mutually exclusive.

As I have informed you, he demonstrated signs of excellence while here. My hope was that this would be continued. My fear was that it would be eradicated somewhat by the upheaval. On the other hand, it's all part of being a teacher. Students come, students go. One can't, or rather shouldn't, become emotionally attached. That's easier said than done, I suppose. Especially given the circumstances. Some of our past pupils have stayed in contact with the school and with certain teachers. We encourage a sort of nurturing environment when our students go on to brighter and better things. I think past rectors like to take credit for their success. We all know that this is utter bumpkin, of course.

To my knowledge his father wasn't a wealthy man, he came from what you would call working-class stock. Clem won a scholarship to this school. It's our way of paying lip service to discrimination, you see. Each year-group has two scholarships available to those who, by comparison, are deemed disadvantaged. Each applicant has to write an essay and go through an interview process. Oh nothing special, we simply enquire as to the applicant's motives and try to delve further under the applicant's skin. It's more like an informal chat really. They can be invaluable actually; in the past we have received some wonderful essays from boys, nevertheless when the applicant comes up against the admission committee it can be quickly established that they wouldn't be a suitable candidate for our school at all. We were unanimous with Clem. We believed that not only would he fit in well with the fabric and ethos of the school but he would also enhance it along the way. He had so much to offer, both personally and academically. I think now we are all questioning our decision-making process and our ability to be immune to hoodwinking. Of course, nobody would dare raise the issue, but there were, and are, some knowing looks and gazes within the staff room.

When Clem left the school we were informed that it was for family reasons, in that his father had lost his job and had taken the family to Scotland in order to take up a new position. I think he worked in the sales industry, as a kind of travelling salesman, however, you would need clarification on that. A difficult time for all of us, the man lost his job and, unfortunately, had to take measures to protect his family. And now this. One tends to think what would have happened if the job market had been more secure down these parts. In an ideal world Clem could have conceivably continued his education with us, but, alas, our scholarship doesn't extend to boarding. Perhaps that should be reviewed.

I think he fitted in well when he came here. Obviously he

was different and we are always wary of the problems students in Clem's situation can cause. By that, I mean we have to keep an eye on the students around him. That he doesn't become isolated or ostracized within the class. That the scholarship students are not singled out for special treatment...of course, I am referring to bullying. It is a disease here in the same way as it is in the comprehensive system. Some may say in schools like ours it has significantly profound effects. You see, our students have all the clever psychological attributes to inflict deep-rooted damage upon those they judge inferior to them. It is a terrible affliction that some of those born into money carry with them throughout their lives. One does wish that this affliction, this hubris, will be their eventual downfall. In many cases I am happy to report that it is.

Clem was free of this. Did he suffer at the hands of anyone? One thing for sure about Clem Curran was that he didn't suffer fools; those who tried to spread their bile were quickly and effectively put in their place. Academically, Clem was head and shoulders ahead of his peers. In a sense they revered him. He was the symbol of hope to so many of us; of how you can have personality and intelligence in abundance. Money can't buy everything, you see. Nonetheless, the odd ribbing went on, but nothing too serious or untoward. He was consistent with his temperament. No, I wouldn't have regarded him as calculated; he was a normal young man. No, I wouldn't have regarded him as a loner either, or, for that matter, an extrovert. He kept himself at arm's-length from his peers, but he was sociable and likeable. He knew his direction in life.

Only one incident springs to mind, it really was so insignificant that it isn't worth noting. Clem had to be reprimanded for striking another boy. More of a slap actually, nothing of note as I said. I think the other lad was questioning, firstly, his parentage and, secondly, his sexual orientation. Apparently this had been going on for some time and Clem had hit breaking point, so naturally he lashed out and struck the other boy. You could say his anger superseded his rationale. The comments stopped immediately after the incident. If one questions his actions one has to ask if he was vindicated given the intense and systematic levels of provocation.

My advice, as I have given throughout the years to students who have been victims of such circumstances, some scholars may say unprofessionally so, has been to provide them with two options: one, inform a teacher, which will quite possibly lead to a continuation as well as an escalation of the ribbing, or bullying, if you prefer. Or, two, hit the perpetrator as hard as you can, with or without warning. My belief was that option two would determine that the hounding and discrimination would cease.

Yes, this was advice I offered Clem at the time. He subsequently took up option two. The problems stopped for him and the school environment became a pleasurable one again. While my methods may be construed as somewhat idiosyncratic or maverick I would pose the question, was I wrong? In light of what's occurred you could say my judgment was skewed a touch. I have gone over this time and time again, do I feel some semblance of responsibility for what has occurred? Does that absolve me from what has happened? Concretely, yes. Philosophically, no. Existentially, well on that one I oscillate.

There are, of course, a few areas that require further explanation and clarification; namely, what was the school's role in all of this? Why did no member of staff anticipate, or foresee, the peril ahead? And the girl implicated with Clem, what is her pedigree? What was her motive? No doubt these questions will all be unearthed after a proper and thorough investigation.

Rosie Farrell's Mum's Concern

Don't get me wrong I was delighted when Rosie and Clem became an item. To me it appeared that it wasn't just your usual boyfriend girlfriend high school romance, but a proper relationship. You know, an item.

As a mother you always worry about your family. I only had the one so all my worry was naturally placed onto Rosie. I know it wasn't fair on her, there were times when I tried to take a back seat and let her make her own way, make her own mistakes; but I can tell you when a mother does that and watches from the sidelines it's heartbreaking. I just didn't want to intrude all the time. I thought that if I gave her space to breathe that it would bring us a wee bit closer together.

Yes, in a way I suppose thinking back I *was* jealous of Clem. He was playing the role I wanted to play. The role I should have been playing. Don't take this the wrong way, it wasn't as if I wanted the two of us to sit down and discuss the birds and the bees. Teenagers are no daft these days. They probably know more than I do now. Our Rosie could probably teach me a thing or two. As a parent you often wonder if your child...you know...if they are that way inclined. Especially Rosie. I never heard her talking about boys or having the idea of bringing a guy home. So I admit there were times when I thought that she might be a...you know...a wee bit...I remember crying about it one night because I thought it was such a waste as she is such a gorgeous lassie. But it would have been okay if she had been that way too; I wouldn't have loved her any less. You can imagine how happy I was when Clem came on the scene and they became a real couple. A proper couple. I was genuinely happy for the two of them. It was probably relief I felt more than anything.

I didn't notice anything strange really, but things definitely changed. Some for the better, some for the worse. Well, she seemed happier and was more talkative around the house. More chirpy. But I could tell if they'd had an argument or something. Oh, it was don't go near her then. There was a time when I thought the two of them had broken up as all she did was mope around the house like a funeral goer. It didn't last though. I'd say to her things like, 'Rosie, if there's anything I can do, or if there's anything you want to talk about just say.' Then she would give you the eyes and glare at you. 'What do you know about it?' she'd say. I just left her when she was like that. There was no talking to her. In the space of a couple of hours it could all change though. That's what I found difficult to deal with, all the inconsistencies. I didn't know if I was coming or going. I don't think she did either. Anyway, for one, I was glad she wasn't kicking with the other foot. It all seemed easier in my day.

Then I went the other way and my main concern was that Rosie and Clem were spending far too much time with each other. Don't get me wrong, I was happy for them, but at that age you need other friends around. I didn't want her to become too reliant on him. I used to think stupid things like: what do they find to talk about all the time? That's only because me and my ex used to sit for ages glued to a bloody television screen and say nothing to each other all night then go to bed. And do the same thing the next night. It used to destroy me. But those two were always cackling away or 'discussing' something. Usually music, films or other stuff like that. I felt heart sorry for wee Cora because she was suddenly bombed out. I think that's when I became wary of Clem, not in a bad way, in a motherly way. Well, think about it, he was up here all the way from somewhere down south with no friends, didn't know anyone in Glasgow by all accounts, and here he was spending all his time with our Rosie. Splitting up her and her friends. That's how some folk could have seen it. There was just a time when I thought that he was taking a loan of her; that everything was on his terms: what they spoke about, where they went to, what music they listened to. I was worried that he was having too much control over her. It's not that I didn't like Clem, I had to take care of number one, and that was Rosie. I didn't treat him differently or become overprotective, Rosie would have seen through that in a flash.

There was something about him that didn't sit well with me. Nothing sinister. One of those imperceptible things. To this day I can't put my finger on it, but it was something, you know what I mean? It's hard to explain really, it could have been the way he looked at you...no...no, nothing like that. The way some people have a specific stare that makes others feel uneasy. They call it something, don't they?...That's right, a thousand-yard stare. Clem had one of those. Then at other times I thought to myself, there's no way he's as old as he says he is. Some of the things he'd come out with made me think that he was some old grandad. I didn't understand some of the garbage he spoke, not garbage but all that intellectual talk about books and the like. I couldn't be bothered with it all. He must have thought I was interested, or he was trying to impress me. Young people do that. I did the same when I was young. Trying to impress boyfriends' parents, or brothers and sisters. I was impressed at first but then it grated on me.

No, there's no way I'd have said anything to Rosie. Sure at that time she thought I was the beesneez, I didn't want to spoil that. I suppose you could say that I was being a bit selfish, but I fought bloody hard to get Rosie on my side and, when I had her, there was no way I was going to let anything, or anyone, come between us.

Yes, I stayed quiet. For my own sanity as much as anything else. Look, I couldn't exactly go up to her and say that I don't fully trust your boyfriend. Tell me a mother who does. She'd have only told me to bugger off and mind my own business. I would have done the very same if it was my own mother. I knew where she would have been coming from.

How did I react? Jesus, how would you have expected me to react? When I found out the first thing I thought of was our Rosie and how she was feeling, that was my first thought, protecting my daughter. After I knew she was okay my mind switched to Clem. When I first heard of it all, I just knew he would have been right in the middle of it, I knew it, and I was right...I was right.

Looking back it's easy to see that he was lonely. A wee lonely boy. I feel for his parents, coming up here to make a new life and having to deal with what they're having to deal with now. Poor people. We're all dealing with it really, I suppose. One moment of madness and suddenly there's a succession of victims, who'll be dealing with it for a lifetime.

A mother knows her daughter, and I know our Rosie would never have allowed herself to get caught up in something like that. No way. So I'm pretty confident the whole thing will get resolved as everything comes out in the open. I'm not too worried because they'll find the truth sooner or later. You can't keep anything a secret around here. The thing is I'm sick for our Rosie having to stay in that place and answer question after question, day after day. Even I've had to answer a load of questions, but that poor lassie has been repeating herself over and over again until she's blue in the face.

And where are his parents in all this? That's what I want to know. No matter what happens, when they realise that our Rosie has had nothing to do with it, do you think the people connected to the others will forget about all this? No chance. And they're a bad bad lot, I'll tell you that. We will have no other option other than to move. I've already been on to the council about locating us to the other side of the city, or even to another city. I can't be doing with all the looks and gossiping. To be honest I'll be glad to get out of here. A new start for the both of us, that's what's needed.

Maybe we'll even go to England. Somewhere by the sea. That would be nice.

Rosie Farrell's Period

I was standing in the cubicle, the last one as you come in the door, it's nearer the window, and it's the cleanest by a mile, and I'm changing my tampon when I hear this faint sound of 'Rosie.' I said nothing. Then another whisper/shout of 'Rosie.' It was Clem. I froze. Then one more 'Rosie.' I mean can a girl not even change her bloody tampon in peace? This was too much. Next thing I know he was inside the toilets! The girls' toilets. Inside. The flippin girls' toilets. So I totally iced up. Statuesque. Like that game we played as weans. I could hear him checking the doors. I sat on the seat and put my feet up to the door, careful not to make a sound. My red Diadoras ready to block any entry. Or boot him full force in the balls if he dared try to enter. My red Diadoras covering the first and last words of the phrase CORA KELLY'S SEEN MORE JAPSEYES THAN AN ORIENTAL OPTICIAN. Poor Cora. ELLY'S SEEN MORE JAPSEYES THAN AN ORIENTAL OP sounded much better.

I could feel my heart beating faster and faster, which made me even more nervous in case it revealed my position. More whispers. Whispers. Whispers. The idiot was pure making all these mad whispering noises as if he was talking to himself. I listened carefully and realised what he was doing was reading all the graffiti on the doors. I heard *The Smiths* being read. He'd know that that was my handiwork. I didn't want him to see his influence staring right at him. Validating him.

My legs were shaking so I had to release them. God, I was so unfit. Bugger it, if he'd peeked over it was his funeral. I could have had him frogmarched out of this school with a blanket lobbed over his dome for perv actions in a flash. I could have screamed rape, sodomy, burglary, anything. I had him by the short and curlies. Then just as I pulled my red trainers off the door and relaxed them on the smelly floor the main door swung open. And what did the bold Clem do? He only shot into the cubicle. Clem shot into the cubicle next to mine. I could make out his breathing. I gave a wee hee hee to myself. That's what you get arsehole! The sound of heels clicked off the floor. I could tell they were cheapo shoes. The click was a cheapo click. Instinct. Probably Primark or Dunnes. They clicked into the cubicle next to Clem's, two down from me. The Mamas and the Papas go to the bog. I was quiet mama. Clem was terrified papa.

The sound of the knickers being taken down sounded familiar. Please don't be a shite. I kept saying in my head. Then the pssssshhhhh sound started. Music to my ears. It was a relief. I imagined what Clem was thinking during all of this. Was he finding all this arousing? The thing is, and this is the totally pure weird thing, I recognised the sound of that piss. I wasn't buzzing. I did. If memory served me right it was the bold Cora in there. It was Cora. Defo. It was confirmed when she didn't wash her hands (Cora for some reason never washed her hands) and left humming that dire Oasis song *Wonderwall*, which she loved. She always hummed because her voice sounded like a dog ripping a couch apart.

As soon as Cora left the toilet Clem scarpered as well. I breathed a huge sigh of relief. I put the thing inside me and flushed away the old one that had been floating in the water all that time. I washed up and bolted out of there. I figured I'd go find Cora and tell her how her piss sounded. Tell the minging cow to wash her hands after touching her fandan as well. She wouldn't be that difficult to find. Then I had another great art project idea, I thought I could do something on toilet graffiti, questioning the salacious (a Clem word) writings with a more subtle and positive type of graffiti art. A kind of Banksy for the school generation. I could have had the good things written on the left wall, and the bad things on the right wall of the cubicle. I'd call it toilet tennis. Brilliant idea! Was it too late to change? I put it out of my mind for the time being. So I shifted out of the bogs and bumped into this pure weirdo of a wee lassie. A future NED in the making.

'Ir you Rosie Farrell?'

'Who wants to know?'

'Ir you Rosie Farrell or no?' she barked back. 'It's a simple question.'

'Aye, what of it?'

'That Inglish guy is lookin fur ye.'

'Clem?'

'Aye, that's it. The guy wey the funny name.'

'Where did you see him?'

'He wiz hangin roon the fird- an fourff-year lassies' bogs.'

'What did he say?'

'Nuffin, jist asked if ye where in there. Seemed desperate.'

'For the toilet?'

'Naw, fur you.'

'Where is he now, any idea?'

'Naw.'

'Well, thanks anyway.'

'Ah heard that he wiz shaggin that inglish teechur?'

'Who?'

'The wan wey the blond hair an big tits.'

'First I heard.'

'Well am telling ye right now.'

'Who told you?'

'Haven't a Scooby.'

'Your arse you don't.'

'Don't get wide,' she said. This was a definite contender for the future queen of the NEDs.

'Where is he now?'

'Witz he doin hanging aroon the girls bogs fur in the first place?'

'Dunno, you'd better ask him that.'

'Pure weirdo if ye ask me, man.'

'Anyway, what way did he go?'

'Haven't a Scooby.'

'Well that's a big help.'

'I just thought a'd tell ye he wiz lookin fur you.'

'Okay, cheers.'

'A heard that Fran McEvoy was goin tae kick the shite oot ay him iz well.'

'Well you heard wrong, didn't ye?'

'Touchy.'

'Shouldn't you be in class anyway?'

'Aye, so?'

'What class are you in?'

'Haven't a Scooby.'

'There's a surprise,' I said. 'Well, whatever your name is, it was nice talking to you.'

'Aye, whitivir. Nae bother.'

I headed off but before I turned to go down another corridor she shouted back at me.

'It's Izzy.'

'What?'

'Ma name's Izzy, by the way.'

'Good for you,' I said. But that wee lassie pure freaked me out. All those things she said about Clem. I knew it was all too good to be true. I knew something would get in the way. Or someone. I was dead realistic about it in my own head. Even during the times when we were getting on like John and Yoko there was always this thing pure nipping away at my head and telling me that a bomb was about to explode. If truth be known, I was a bit pissed off that I just couldn't get on with enjoying the whole thing instead of always thinking negative thoughts. That was dead annoying. It made me really defensive and on edge. I don't think I was a good person to be around at that time. The whole Croal thing was nothing by comparison. Nothing.

But there's only my word for it.

Cora Kelly Talks About Her Musical Taste...in a Roundabout Way

A wiz the last one to see Rosie before it all happened and I'll tell you what, if she wiz going to do anything she would have told me first. As her best mate she would have. No danger.

And if she didn't say anything, which she didn't, I would have spotted something a mile off anyway. No danger.

She wiz just the same Rosie that day apart from having women's problems, which we all have, and we all have a pure mad off day, but nothing that would lead us to that. No danger.

The thing that made her really annoyed that day wiz Clem. He wiz acting like a pure rocket. I always thought he wiz a smart arse. He thought he wiz pure cool as and dead good-looking. Pure lookin down his nose at us coz he thought he wiz this pure big brainy guy.

He warped her mind. After she met him she started listenin to all this mad music, you know that type of music that messes with the head. You just need to look at what's happened in America because of that mad music people listen to. Loads of people get killed in schools over there, don't they? And in Germany as well! No, I'm not blaming it *all* on the music. Anyway, she wiz one of those people that didn't believe in all that stuff, she wiz a pacific person. Eh? Someone who believes in peace and all that. A pacifist, whatever.

The last time I saw her wiz in the toilets. They wouldn't let anyone see her, apart from her maw.

Conor Duffy Offers Insight

A told him from day one. Stay well away man. Don't go anywhere near them. But a suppose all that guff aboot him and Miss Croal brought them tae him more than the other way aroon. All a kin say is that he must have been pure mad with the rage when it happened. His heed must have been mush by that stage. Rid mist ivrywhere. Pure mad as, man. Pure mad as! Thir wir hunners ay lassies greetin their eyes out when they heard. Some guys as well. A heard thit Rosie's maw wiz movin tae a different area. A think that's fir the best. Specially roon here.

You don't know wit tae believe, do you? You hear all sorts. Big Liam knows a guy whose brother knows a guy who works doon at the polis station. Anyway, who knows? All you hear is one story after another. All ay them as mince as the nixt. A'm no speaking ill ay anyone, but it wiz just a matter ay time.

Rosie's the one a feel sorry fir. Heart sorry fir the lassy. She didnay deserve that.

Mr Cunningham's Boxed Up Version of Passion

Maybe, just maybe, Rosie Farrell's subterfuge to regain the affections of her boyfriend went askew and the subsequent consequences of this led to these appalling events. A crime of passion you could say. Who knows what goes through the mind of a teenager scorned? God knows I don't and I have been teaching for a many number of years. We are still learning new things from week to week in this job. It would be prudent for Pauline Croal to remember this fact. At the end of the day, however, what this is is a damn shame and nothing more. It's something that could have quite easily leapt from the pages of a Shakespearean tragedy.

Of course, our school has organised counselling sessions for both our staff and pupils. Collectively we have to move on and learn the lessons of the event.

Rosie Farrell Gets Something off Her Chest

No, I didn't go. There was no way I was going to that class. I knew that I'd pass my exams. I didn't need to work with a group of nerds talking about poems and Shakespeare and all that crap. It wasn't as if I was going to study English when I left school…I wanted to go to art college or study design or architecture or something like that. I don't know really. But I knew I wasn't going to spend my time at uni or college reading these pure mad thick books though.

It was nothing to do with the fact that Miss Croal was taking the study group. I had no real opinion about her. She just got to me. You know, rubbed me up the wrong way.

There was one time I went to school dead early. The janny had to open the doors for me. That's how early it was. I wanted to make a start on my art project. So I'm standing there looking at the Miró calendar that I've brought in with me in order to draw out the inspiration I need. All that arty farty cack. Reflection, emotional memory and all that tosh. I bought the Miró calendar a few weeks ago in an art shop in town, at first I was going to give it to Clem as a wee 'welcome to Glasgow' present but I just kept it for myself. He could stick to his bands. It would have been inappropriate to give him a calendar of a Spanish artist as a welcome to Glasgow anyway. And there was no way I was giving him a Jack Vettriano. He's dire.

So I'm standing there like a lemon in the middle of this big empty art room waiting for the god of art to come and scud me full force on the face. There wasn't a soul about. Not a sound could be heard. Then I heard something in the yard. A click clicking sound. I look out of the window and see Miss Croal making her way through the yard wearing these heels. Not exactly stilettos but high enough to make an echo. I remember thinking: 'she's keen.' And then thinking how she's dressed like a slapper for school. If that's what she's jumping into on a Tuesday morning, I wouldn't like to see her on the weekend. Who's she out to impress? I didn't give it another thought until I hear the same click clicking sound walking up the long corridor outside the art rooms. She had to walk that way to get to the English base. And then, all of a sudden, the clicking slows to long pauses between steps. Close to where I was. My mind was full of garbage art ideas: leeks for hair, broccoli noses, zucchini fingers and other rubbish plans, when the sound stops. Just like that. As if dead.

Then I hear voices. Voices that are trying to be quiet so that people won't detect anything or eavesdrop. Am like, 'who the fuck is that?' to myself. So curiosity killed the cat, and all that, and I try and sneak a peek. And, honestly, no word of a lie it's Clem and Croal. Sharing idle chit-chat? Just talking? No way, Jose. She had her hand on his face. On his face! As if caressing him. The slut! The bastards! Then she moved closer to him, and I swear I thought she was going to plank the lips full on him. I really did. I was clocking all this from a wee hole in the poster that covered the glass part of the door. I was ready to rip the door down and make a beeline for the pair of them. Kicking and screaming. My blood was boiling. I was ready to rip that door down and rip the head off the both of them. He keeps turning around to see if anyone's looking. And I'm like 'ya fuckin prick' behind the door. Whispering it through gritted teeth. My breathing got heavier and I felt the sweat starting to form on my dome.

She looked worried as if they'd had a row or something and then she made a move on his face again.

Same hand.

Same part of the face.

This was a dangerous game they were playing.

In the corridor during school time!

I could have had the slag's job on a plate.

I held it in the palm of my hand.

Her career.

Her life.

I could have made some serious dosh with the papers. *The Sun* would print any old crap, made up or not. Thinking back, it's mad to think that I had the power. One click with the moby and her tea was out. Goodnight Vienna. And so was his. No more Brighton. No more dreams of beaches. What a pair of bastards. Did they not think anyone would have found out? What a pair of complete eejits. Maybe the NEDs had the right idea after all. Then the touching stopped and they moved on, in separate directions. I think they heard something, or someone, coming. Probably Clem in his pants.

Put it this way he was *no* Olympic champion in that department. I could have strangled him. I was pure hyperventilating behind the door. I wanted to scream out loud. Just let it all out. I hated Croal. I fucking hated her fucking guts. Her and her figure and her brains and her eyes and her lips. I hated everything about her. I wanted to kick the life out of the art room, boot all the easels around. Smash up all the work in the class. Pull it down off the walls. Students' work over the years. All the good stuff. Launched out of the window. That was him finished. But I had to compose myself. I took it in through the nose and out through the mouth. I stuck the *Yeah Yeah Yeahs* on the CD player and blasted it. Loud. Then it suddenly came to me. The inspiration for my art project. I'd do portraits of sluts, slappers and slags. An abstract representation of course. Thanks, Miss Croal.

When the break came I couldn't find him. I looked everywhere. Asked around. I even wandered up to that bitch Croal's class to see if their wee rendezvous was continuing. I went out to the smokers knowing full well that he wouldn't be out there. I hated him for making me worried.

But I can rationalise it now. In that moment, in that art room, I hated Croal. Hated her with everything I had. But I kept it to myself. That's why it's bonkers when everyone says I always hated her! Why does everyone say that? That's what confuses me. They know zilch. Just because I didn't get a movement in my pants when she spoke to me, like most of the guys, or wish to be like her, like most of the girls, doesn't mean I hated her. She was full of herself. And she was a flirt, I don't care what anyone says, she was. She would do that thing where she would pure stare at guys for ages when she asked them a question without blinking, it gave me and Cora the heebies. It was like she was trying to seduce them with her eyes. Then she'd come in with these really tight tops on to show off her boobs. It was pure sad as anything.

85

So what if Clem liked her? He's allowed to like teachers, we're allowed to disagree on certain things. Not that we did disagree on it. We didn't disagree on much. He liked her but he didn't grovel over her like all the other guys. That time in the corridor she was touching his face, his eye. It was all bruised. Looked like he'd been shoved in a washing machine on full spin. She was concerned. That's what I clung onto. The two of them went on all the time about books and writers and all these poets that I'd never even heard of. English was his favourite subject after all. He told her he wanted to write books when he was older. I think she was impressed by that... I think she was impressed by Clem in any case. Probably stuck her boobs in the air to show it too. I'd no interest in that stuff; I got bored writing a two-page essay. If you told Mr Cunningham that you wanted to write books he'd probably laugh at you, I suppose she was good in that respect. Look, it's not as if we spent our whole time talking about Miss Croal or anything. We'd better things to talk about, you know.

End Of Part One

Part Two

What Clem Said

Moving

When your mother says, 'look at the state of those sheets', she doesn't really mean that your bed sheets are dirty and thus require a high temperature wash (well she does in a roundabout way) but rather, bed is no place for masturbating and the bed sheets are definitely no place to clean the testicular muck.

I didn't have the *talk* about puberty, onanism, hormones, lust, etc. Even love for that matter. Instead I was left to fend for myself. Set adrift in an otherwise hedonistic landscape, floating and bobbing away through one experience after another. Good and bad. I made a multitude of mistakes along the way: kissing like a washing machine on speed, groping around the upper torsos of many females with wild abandon (to the onlooker, or purist, they would have sworn in a court of law that an actual sexual assault had been taking place) and placing hands, and fingers, in places so unfamiliar that it was as uncomfortable for me as it was for the recipient. Blame it on my naivety. Or my parents.

Although being at the tender age of sixteen, I have a superfluity of future mistakes to make in this area. More than anything now, I hope so. Superfluity is my new word. In fact, it's the first time I have used it in context. Not sure if I have used it properly. I'll give myself the benefit of the doubt. And where was this little gem of a word introduced to me? Mr Goldsmith's English class. Where else?

'I've finished that book you gave us, Sir.'

'All of it?'

'Well, I got to the last page.'

'In that case I'd suggest choosing another.'

'I've actually had a look and they are not that great.'

'Really, Mr Curran?'

'Afraid so, Sir.'

'Oh nonsense, I'm sure we have a superfluity of books that would suit both your taste and appetite.'

And that's how the word superfluity was born and introduced into my vocabulary. I'd like to do Mr Goldsmith justice. He'd be proud of me. What has all this got to do with anything? Nothing in particular. I am trying to hold on to memories. The issue with the sheets happened on that morning I was informed of our trip to Scotland.

Scotland!

To be precise: 'Glasgow.'

Glasgow!

Even though mum already knew about it she looked as shocked as I was. In fact I was the one who was shocked, she was only stunned. I'd snap out of it. I had the distinct feeling that she'd take much longer to leave her stunned state. I was still coming to terms with the embarrassment of the sheets incident, hoping that nothing more would be said about it. I was dreading the imminent scene when walking home from school that night. I had played it over and over in my head and could foresee a painful conversation between father and son. Me nodding feebly at his feeble efforts of analogy. A feeble fusion. That was all I needed. Now it seemed some-

thing was pushing this fear into a wilderness of insignif-
icance, which I was eternally grateful about. Actually *grateful*
no; delighted, yes. I wiped the sweat from my brow and let
out a loud phew! All in my head of course, I wouldn't be so
explicit. And then the implications hit home.

Glasgow? Why Glasgow? Of all the places we could have
gone to, which I'm led to believe were none, why on this earth
would someone choose to go to Glasgow? It's not that I have
anything against the Scots, or Glaswegians, as a people or a
nation, it's just, well, Eastbourne is so much not Glasgow. On
the surface, they seem like the complete antithesis of each
other. To someone, that is, who has no perception. That's
before you even consider the clichés. What would I do in
Glasgow? What would we do in Glasgow? Why the hell are
we going to Glasgow? What the hell is there for people like us
in Glasgow? Won't we be hounded out of the place? Again
never said, all in the head.

'It's work, Clem,' dad said.

'It's your father's work, Clem,' mother reiterated.

'But you have a job here,' silence. 'Don't you have a job
here?' Prickly silence, almost embarrassingly so. 'Do you have
a job here or not?'

'I do, but the company is downsizing.'

'So you don't have a job?' I said.

'It's a sign of the times, Clem. The economic situation,'
mum said, in his defence. Suddenly it all became apparent: it
was me against them. And why does everyone blame their
own shit on the 'economic situation'? Why can't people take

responsibility for their own actions? I didn't ask to be born in to this blah blah blah…immature brat thing…blah blah blah.

'I do have a job, it's just not the same job I had here.'

'So you've been demoted,' I said.

'Oh, please don't use that word, Clem. Your father has found a different position in a difficult job market that's all. We should be happy for him.'

'Difficult job market?' Christ, is this the level my unfulfilled housewife mother is functioning at? She'll be quoting the Dow Jones and Keynesian recovery practices next. I was still in shock, I guess. The word Glasgow buzzing around my head.

'We should be happy for him?'

Oh, I'm ecstatic.

'Look Clem, it's the company offering me a similar position to the one I had here. They're closing down their operation in Eastbourne, but not in Glasgow.'

'So we have no choice?' I said.

'We have no other choice, I'm afraid,' dad said.

'Have you looked?' I said.

'Of course your father has looked,' mother said. 'What do you think we are, impulsive?'

'Heaven forbid,' I said.

'We have no option,' dad said.

'So it's settled?' I said.

'It's settled,' dad said.

'We have no choice,' mum said.

'When?' I said.

'Next weekend,' mum said.

'Next weekend?' I said.

'Next weekend,' dad said.

'What about school?' I said.

'We have found a super school in Glasgow,' dad said.

'Does such a thing exist?' I said.

'Don't be sarcastic, Clem,' mum said.

'So we leave our sense of humour here as well? Can I at least pack mine?' I said.

'Clem this is difficult for everyone concerned, let's make it more bearable than it already is,' dad said.

'Can I not finish off the last year here?' I said.

'No,' dad said.

'Out of the question,' mum said. 'The market is forcing us. It simply wouldn't allow it.'

There she goes again.

'Next weekend?' I said.

'Next weekend,' dad said.

'It'll be fine Clem, we'll settle in quickly up there, you wait and see,' mum said. 'I hear the people are really friendly.'

'Yeah, I hear that they have the highest rate in knife crime in Europe,' I said.

'Let's think positively,' dad said.

'Exactly,' mum said. 'And who knows maybe the banks will get their act together quicker than we imagine.'

'Yeah, fingers crossed, eh?' I said, raising both hands and crossing my fingers. It didn't end there, but it's so tedious and unimportant that this point is the best place to cut it off. After boring me to near mental meltdown I reeled off to my room to begin the packing process. At least my sheets were fresh.

So that was it. That's how unpredictable life can be as a teenager. Nevertheless, I was thankful for a few things. First, I was thankful that the sheet incident was dead and buried. The message had been received loud and clear. I swore never to allow myself to be open to such humiliating criticism again. Always use the bathroom for these kinds of activities, unless, that is, you live alone, there is mutual consent or you can be sure that no one will go near your bed in order to change the bedding, like a flatmate etc. Second, I was glad I wasn't leaving a girlfriend back in Eastbourne; the emotional baggage would have been too much to bear. I wouldn't have wanted to cart it around Glasgow with me. I was happy there was nobody special in my life. Third, I needed a change of scenery, Eastbourne was destroying my desire and I needed to get out of there. This was the perfect opportunity. Oh I had to still play up to the tempestuous teenager tag, it's an adolescent duty. They'll sleep with their guilt and I'll be the beneficiary.

Strangely enough I was delighted by my father's inadequacies in the job market. He had had a variety of jobs in my time of understanding what working and employment actually meant. All his jobs were in and around the south coast so it didn't seem like the world had shifted when he 'moved on'. I always thought he did something special and important because he wore a shirt and tie. I suspect he did, too. How wrong I was. There's no escaping the fact that throughout his working life he'd been a floater, a human frog hopping from one shit job to another. This time however he had outdone himself. That's not to suggest that I wasn't sensitive to his and mum's plight, I was. But in equal measure I was sensitive to the fact that I didn't want to portray the little prick of teenage impertinence for too long either. On the contrary, I was happy to view Glasgow as an experiment. Bring it on! Given that the life expectancy of the UK male is seventy-seven I had another sixty-one years of living to look forward to. Notwithstanding luck with accidents. One year spent in Glasgow wasn't going to crush my plans for world domination.

I called my dad Willy Loman. Not to his face. I said it in my head. Just me and my head. As soon as we read ten pages of *Death of a Salesman* and Mr Goldsmith began to talk about the protagonist, all I could think of was dad dressed in Willy's clothes, saying his lines and eating his food. In a flash it all became apparent, dad was the embodiment of Willy Loman, in soul and spirit. Chasing something that was unattainable. The poor bastard. Selling factory to factory, shop to shop, door to door, man to man, day to day, year to year is enough to break the strongest of men. My dad, like Willy, was broken.

97

At least Willy had the gumption to have himself an affair, get some fun along the way before his downfall. Dad, on the other hand, was weak willed, let people walk all over him, allowed himself to be given orders, to be undermined and humiliated by recent sharp-suited graduates with no sense of anything other than themselves. I fucking hated those graduates. But what a state to get into nevertheless; the poor, pathetic bastard. If ever there was a motivation to learn from your parents' mistakes... One thing for sure, none of those graduates were breaking their balls selling for their feed, no, they were too busy sucking the devil's cock in order to fatten their wallets. None of those graduates were half the man my dad was. None of those graduates were going to Glasgow.

Glasgow

You don't get the feel of anything from the back seat of a car. The back seat symbolises the least important person in the car. And us driving to Scotland symbolised the least important person in dad's company. There was no conversation to be had because the music, which was just barely discernible in the front, blared in the back. It happens in cheap cars. Therefore we didn't get beyond the 'can you turn that down a bit, please?' level of conversation. Reading was out of the question in case I projected vomit over the back of mum's brand spanking new demi-wave. I'm a bad traveller. Everything just whizzed past in series of greys, greens and whites. I fixed my eyes on a dead fly stuck to the window; the car was filthy. It could have been worse, that fly could have been me. I was alive and raring to go.

The M6 was as far North as I had ever been in England. For some reason I could tell it was the north I was travelling through. You hear stories about the divide, usually perpetrated by the south's snobbery about the north, but I have to say the further north I travelled the duller it got. Forty, or even twenty years ago the sky would have been dark from the furnaces, the chimneys, the work, now it was just grey from rain clouds. Zooming up the M6, towards Scotland, even the sheep looked to have an air of resignation about them: a foreboding sense of what was north of that border. They knew, they had sheep family in Scotland. And then the sign: *Welcome to Scotland* approached us. Or, rather, we approached it. We gave a collective cheer, more out of ritual than joy. Then we all reverted into the recesses of our minds and secretly, I'll bet, thought: *Christ Almighty!* I did anyway. As soon as we entered Scotland, or left England, (whatever way you want to look at it) the signs for Glasgow came thick and fast.

It took about an hour for us to escape rural Scotland. After which there was no doubt that we were within touching distance of Glasgow. High-rise flats could be seen far in the distance, like monolithic military men standing to attention, closely watching our every move. Protecting us as we advanced, overseeing our every movement, maybe. The welcome was intimidating. I wondered how many people were crammed into this place. What clever architectural mind was behind such atrocities? What illicit activities go on in and around these colossal concrete structures? What life flies by inside the tiny boxes that formed them? This was a proper city with proper city fixtures. It was a million miles from Eastbourne. It smelt different, felt colder. In the back of that car it seemed like a million miles away from us too. As we took in our new surroundings not one word was uttered between us. *Bloody Hell's Fire...Oh, God Save Us...Shit* couldn't exactly be heard but it was tangibly floating around the car nonetheless. Until mum broke it.

'Well, here we are.'

'Yup,' dad said.

'It's big,' mum said.

'Yup.'

'A bit different from Eastbourne,' she said, trying to make light.

'Yup.'

I wanted to slap the back of his head.

'I'm sure they'll be lots of record and bookshops, Clem,' mum said.

'Yeah, can't wait?' I said, immediately cursing my immaturity. I wanted to slap my own head.

'Well, they'll be lots more to do, that's all I'm saying.' I loved my mother in that instance. I apologised to her in my head. She hadn't bought into this crap. I knew this wasn't her dream sitting next to her with his hands stuck on the steering wheel. Motionless.

Emotionless.

She smiled, remained positive, kept her own counsel and failed to allow Glasgow's grey cloud to descend. I needed to be more like her. Stuff all that chip-off-the-old-block shit. It wasn't for me. I was a mummy's boy. She was the one I felt sorry for. The one I aspired to be like. He could escape and do what he does everyday...make a living. I had school. What did she have? If it wasn't for me, would she have been sitting in this car in the first place? Or, would she have realised the error of her ways and made a quick exit? Did she secretly blame me for her situation?

Driving to our new home, in the south-east of the city, led us through a succession of downcast faces and expressions. There was uniformity about the buildings, solid tenement structures everywhere. The hard buggers of the housing world. The elements didn't mess with these guys. They imposed their will upon the city, dwarfing the street activity below. One of these tenement flats was to be our new home.

Monday

Obviously it wasn't my decision to come up here. As young people we're just told where and when to go. Slaves to the parents, man. Well, you hear all these stories about Glasgow, don't you? Knives, sectarianism, gangs, violence, Buckfast for breakfast, rain. All that clichéd rubbish. If truth be known, I welcomed the adventure. Anthropology. I figured I wasn't going to be here that long anyway. A year max. Max!

Then back down south, not Eastbourne though. No way. Brighton maybe. Who knows, right? I knew I could stick a year. I'm not a problem child or anything like that.

The thing that tickled me was the accent. I thought it was brilliant, full of character, sheer energy. It does sound like one big constant argument taking place all over the city though. I'm still trying to get to grips with it. I'd say that for one in four people I have met, I haven't a clue what they are saying. I just nod my head to them. The Pakistanis are sound though. Up here they have this cool accent that blends the Glaswegian and Pakistani accent. Vocal melody. Music to the ears around these parts.

It was the noise that was the big difference. It came in all directions swirling through every corridor attacking my ears. It was not a distinguishable noise. I'd go as far as saying that I hadn't a clue what was being said around me. All the voices blended into this huge imperceptible din. And then, of course, the staring. I had prepared myself for this. The realisation that I was new. The spanking new boy. That day's difference. That day's talking point. In my paranoia all eyes were on me, shaking me down, checking me out. Girls asking themselves the question: would they or wouldn't they? Guys asking: Who the hell is that? Is he competition? Could I take him in a scrap? The iPod was loaded. Blocking everything out.

I wasn't concerned that I had no friends. I knew that there would be a transition period, but, really, I didn't need any friends. My plan was simple, keep the head down, get the grades and get out. Get to a good uni. Not unreachable. I'm not saying I would close myself off to the possibility of meeting new people, but I'm not really into what's going on right now: computer games for a start, Play Stations, Xboxes, Facebook, My Space, Twitter, downloading ringtones, getting all the cool apps for whatever phone is in vogue. All that crap. I'm old school in my new school. I watch films, read books, listen to music, play my guitar. Nothing special.

I used to play rugby at my old school, you had no choice really, but I wouldn't say I was, like, Mr Sports Fan, either. I appreciated that I may not have been the life and soul for other lads my age. I wasn't appealing. People wouldn't clamber to be around my sharp and witty diatribes. I'm not good friend material.

The place was like a town in itself. A maze of corridors and doors. I was lost. I flicked on the iPod and searched for *Meat is Murder*, I blasted *The Headmaster's Ritual* into my ear. How apt, I thought. I plonked myself in a secure spot in the school's foyer and took in my new surroundings. Were the students in this place of learning that different from those in my last school? Actually, yes they were. For starters they had girls here. Lots of girls. Now, I wouldn't say that on first glance the school was undisciplined but a quick scan of what was before me unearthed puerile scurrying, hostile harrying, pushing and shoving, the odd spit, dead arms, slaps on the head, vocal vandalism and bag throwing. In my last school, there was an eerie hush at this time in the morning; all students were expected to walk in the one direction down the halls and corridors. Military style. *Dead Poets' Society* style. Draconian style. Uniforms were immaculately worn. Collars starched. Trousers pressed. However, I much preferred the dress code here. I liked that many students had artistically altered the original, it said a lot about the place. The people. Although saying that, many didn't wear a uniform, favouring instead the uniform of the chav: the tracksuit and hat amalgamation. Abomination. The more self-aware stylishly tucking their tracky bottoms into their white socks...nice. Maybe I'd alter my uniform too. Maybe I'd go crazy and undo my top button or something more radical like turn my tie around to the thin side. What an iconoclast! Hold on to your seats.

Then there were the conspicuous groupings: geeks, rockers, goths, *Kaiser Chiefs'* fans (and groups of a similar ilk), Topman/Topshop/H&M/River Island clones, etc. etc. I sat there thinking what grouping this school would thrust me into; who'd label me first. For sure, I wanted to be in a minority group. A minority group of one: the English Geezer Group. I suspected the word 'geezer' was a no-no however. The English Twat Group. That sounded like a good group to me. How many folk listened to *The Smiths* in this school? How many people knew who they actually were?

I had never seen so many girls in the one place, not all at

the same time anyway. Especially this time on a Monday morning, with an intriguing array of styles and sizes...and attractiveness. I didn't consider myself unattractive, nor particularly attractive for that matter, but being new in a school did have a certain weight of allure about it. Perhaps the accent could weave its way into some girl's heart. Or more. After all, I had to concentrate on the positives. Plural.

School

I never know how many steps you should take, or how many seconds to count in your head, before you turn around to look at someone passing you by. The last thing you want to do is to turn at the same time and catch each other's eye. You want to avoid that awkward pause, which seems to last an eternity, before you flick your eyes off to something else, a place so incongruous to the reason for turning around in the first place. As much as I wanted to, I didn't turn around. I gazed from a distance. Stared from the security of a class back seat. Gawked behind a sandwich in the canteen.

Each day was an exercise in voyeurism, but that's what being a hormonal teenager in school is all about, is it not? This was frustrating as well because I became all too (un)aware who was available and who was out of bounds. The last thing I wanted to do was to put anyone's nose out of joint. Not least my own. It's not as though I craved a girlfriend or anything, I was simply playing out my role as a teenager. Horny and on the prowl. A teenage prowl, not a perverted one.

For the first time in my life I felt isolated. Even though it was only to last for a few weeks, it took its toll. I began to loathe the idea of going to that school. Every waking moment away from the place was spent on reading or plucking my guitar, whereas at school I played catch-up. Academically the work wasn't too taxing. I coped admirably. It was easy street. Unlike the work, I found the school to be somewhat problematic at first; no one spoke to me, welcomed me, inquired as to where I was from, invited me to join them at lunch, commented on my accent, took the piss out of me. Nothing. I was invisible. In the music class I couldn't even get my hands on a guitar. I was too far down the pecking order. I had to endure awful renditions of *Oasis, The Fratellis* and *The* bloody *Kooks* while I sat tapping away on a shabby keyboard. On numerous occasions I'd amble around the place and sense that people were staring at me, talking about me, even intrigued by me, but I wanted more. There were many clumsy moments when there was an unavoidable coming together in corridors, yet eyes would make a sudden flick to the side, heads would suddenly aim for the floor or, worse, there would be a boorishly impulsive change of direction. In my paranoia it felt like the entire school was compliant in its endeavour to exclude me, including the teachers. It was like being the only white person at a Black Panther's AGM...or something like that.

Like I said, it was my paranoia more than the reality. Nevertheless I couldn't help but feel disappointed by the behaviour surrounding me; before arriving in Glasgow I took solace in the fact that Scottish people, and particularly, Glaswegians were a friendly and tolerable bunch. Not on this evidence they weren't. On the flip side, my dad said that he was having 'a great time in his new job and couldn't be happier with his new colleagues'. I didn't believe him.

Language

I noticed Rosie after a couple of days. We were in the same classes for English, Italian and Religion. She didn't display any great flair for the subjects I have to say, that's not to suggest that I found her unintelligent. Uninterested would be more accurate. She was quiet in the classes. She spoke only when the teachers asked her to. There was something different about her; she stood out from the other girls. By a mile. I have racked my brain as to what made her stand out so much and concluded that it wasn't really her look that cast her aside, although it did play a significant part in it, but rather her attitude and general demeanour.

When I first noticed her she had this look on her face, a look that suggested she was having a bad day. Snarly almost. It was a real don't-mess-with-me kind of expression. That look alone made her more exciting and interesting in an instance. She had more going on behind those eyes of hers than anyone else. She gave the impression that she thought the guys in the school were humdrum, immature and tedious. My embryonic experience wouldn't have challenged her on this. I hadn't seen too many hanging around her so my belief was that her would-be suitors had understood clearly her don't-even-bloody-think-about-it aura.

Rosie reminded me of the Ally Sheedy character in *The Breakfast Club*. Sheedy played the dark mysterious one with the sultry eyes, cool clothes and independent taste in music. I remember when a few of the lads at my last school watched it for the first time everyone was raving about Molly Ringwald's character, the sweet, innocent, girl-next-door type. Let's be honest, she was attractive in her own way but not anything to write home about. Not to mention the red hair. I was in the Ally Sheedy camp. Rosie reminded me of Ally Sheedy, only a much better-looking version. In a way she reminded me of home.

I never approached Rosie for fear of rousing the passions of others and because I wasn't in the mood for any kind of rejection. I didn't wish to start my new school with a humiliating cloud hovering over me. Folk sneering from afar. It's not as if I was playing it cool either. What I was doing was innocently admiring a girl from a safe distance. I suppose it all started in that Italian class:

'Rosie, you pair up with Clem,' silence from both of us. My heart sped up. 'I'll give you five minutes or so to go through the handout on 'directions'.' My heart picked up the pace. 'If you want, you can veer away from the handout and ask for directions here in Scotland, or where Clem is from.' My heart was sprinting. 'Where are you from again, Clem?'

'Eastbourne, Miss.' I was wondering why she had inserted 'again' into her question.

'How lovely. Okay, get on with it.' I shifted chairs.

'Hi. I'm Clem,' what else could I have said?

'Rosie,' she said, all curt and cute.

'Listen, Rosie I'm not that hot at Italian, I only crashed it last year, at my other school. If I make any mistakes please forgive me.'

'Well I'm completely shite at it, so I wouldn't know if you

were making any mistakes anyway.'

'Okay, shall we start?'

'Go ahead, amigo.'

'That's Spanish.'

'What?'

'"Amigo," it's Spanish, not Italian,' I knew it was an inappropriate thing to say. Stupid thing to say. Not cool.

'I knew that. What, do you think I am, pure thick or something?'

'Not at all.'

'Well then.'

'Okay, shall we start again?'

'Okay, on you go…AMIGO.'

'Okay,' I said.

'Right, go.'

'Okay.'

'Fuck sake, GO,' she said. I sucked in some air.

'Scusi, dove è la piazza principale?'

'What?'

'Dove è la piazza principale?'

'Say it in English first.'

'Then it wouldn't be an Italian exercise.'

'Who cares, it's not as if I'll need Italian in these parts

anyway, some people are still perfecting English up here, you know. So Italian would be like a pure foreign language to them.'

I didn't know what to say. I knew by then that I was attracted to this girl. Really attracted to her.

'Yeah, I suppose so.'

'That was a joke, by the way.'

'Oh, of course.'

'God almighty. No sense of humour down where you're from?'

'Sorry I was just admiring your badges. I like the *Bright Eyes* ones.'

'You know *Bright Eyes*?'

'Of course I do. I didn't know you were an emo chick,' I said. Just like that I had said it, without thinking. What a clown! Like why should I have known one way or the other? I had let my guard slip. She'd have known that I was on to her. Keeping an eye on her.

'Who are you calling a fucking Emu?

'No, not an Emu. Emo, it means emotional, like the band's songs. It has nothing to do with the birds.' I was laughing. Her look of perplexity reminded me of Paris Hilton, not that she looked anything like Paris Hilton, thank God. It was just the sheepish way she reverted into herself that's all, like a bimbo. I think she felt it too. Then, instead of doing the role-play, we had a conversation about music and school and students and teachers and just general nonsense.

'You should check out *The Smiths*,' I said.

'Who?'

'You've never heard of *The Smiths*?

'No.'

'*The Smiths* will save your soul,' I said.

'Right, okay, John Peel, don't rub it in, just tell me who they are,' which I did. She told me that she would discover them that very night. Then the class ended. I was gutted.

I knew that the next day she would be eager to tell me that she had just listened to the best band in the world. And, if she hadn't, if she thought they were completely shit, then I knew we were never meant to be. I had consigned myself to it. How could anyone think *The Smiths* were shit? It's a good barometer with which to judge someone. The perfect barometer. Thinking *The Smiths* are shit tells me a lot about a person. Thinking they're brilliant tells me more.

NEDs

When Rosie told me what it actually meant I thought it was absolutely hilarious. We had a comparable demographic in England yet the word chav was nowhere near as inventive as the word NED. You have to applaud the clever use of the acronym. I mean Non-Educated Delinquent is brilliant in capturing everything about them. Classic. It was comical that some actually referred to the term NED to describe themselves. And how correct they were. One of them actually screamed down the corridor at me, 'Don't fuck with the NEDs.' Middle fingers on full display. I didn't believe their referencing the word was self-deprecation; they didn't strike me as being that ironic. NEDs. The name tickled me.

I didn't hate them. Hate wasn't the word I'd use. I certainly disliked them, I even pitied them at one point, but hate would have been too powerful an emotion for me to express. I wouldn't have given any of them the satisfaction of having my hate. I found them benign. More than anything else they annoyed me. That was on a good day when I could actually understand what the hell they were saying...oh, it was the usual thoughtless stuff; it didn't extend beyond sexual preferences, religious bigotry, my clothes or what football team I supported. It was funny because it seemed to vex them more when I informed them that I didn't like football. Apparently this is just not acceptable behaviour in Glasgow. Everyone has to be labelled, tarred or pigeon holed. I refused to be branded in such an infantile way. They categorised me regardless of my beliefs and preferences, however. My first experience of a lose-lose situation.

When all the slagging started I assumed it was because I was English, but I quickly learnt that it wasn't. They viewed me as an easy target. A guy isolated in a big new school, in a big new city. Someone searching to find his way. I was a sitting duck to them. Easy pickings. Fodder.

I didn't say anything in my defence as it was made clear to me in no uncertain terms that I'd be better off ignoring them. We did have a similar level of ignorance, prejudice and intolerance in England; Glasgow didn't have a monopoly on brainless delinquency. I wasn't much of a fighter, but I knew when and where to speak my mind, or to challenge sensibilities. I also wanted to maintain my dignity. What was the point in any case? Was I that special person who was going to ignite the flame of reason in their heads? Were we about to arrive at a common understanding through a succession of long-winded and exhaustive negotiations? No way. Be a man, walk away, takes the bigger and braver man, and all that jargon. Fundamentally I valued my own aesthetic too much to step over that line.

It started pretty much as soon as I arrived in the school, give or take a few days here or there. It wasn't something I was used to in my last school. If anything problematic occurred it was settled rapidly through fisticuffs, or one swift fisticuff. That's how I settled it in the past. An old teacher told me to belt the bully if he was becoming too tiresome. I did. We played rugby at my last school, so you could say there was an inherent level of aggression that permeated. And, in many ways, an honour to settling scores with fists. However, I didn't think I would have taken on that advice here. That past, that experience, seemed like a lifetime ago.

I was thankful that Rosie was around. Not that I used her because I was getting a hard time. She was my girlfriend and we were together. Hard time or not, we would have still been together. Another thing to remember: I wasn't singled out. They harangued the life out of most folk. At a rough guess there were about ten of them. Sometimes there would be just a handful. They were always in numbers and always a threat. I kept saying to myself, *a year up here, tops*. I had a thick skin and was very determined. My determination wouldn't overstretch any boundaries. I was in control of the situation. There was no point approaching a teacher, it's not as if they were oblivious to the situation either, they buried their heads in the sand and pretended that nothing was happening. Anything for an easy-life approach. Probably the reality is that half of them were NED intimidated too, especially the female teachers. They may have found their swanky cars scratched from boot to bonnet had they confronted them.

There were a few comments about Miss Croal. Water off a duck's back. I heard the rumours. It's not as if I wandered around the school like Helen Keller…what could I do? I let them wash over me; I started to realise the moments when to turn my iPod on, block everything out. My main concern was trying to alleviate Rosie's fears. I was also worried that Miss Croal would be victimised because of what people were saying about her, about us, that the school's superiors would get wind of it and make life difficult for her. In a sense I was thankful that the majority of the defamatory comments came from the NEDs because their opinions and beliefs didn't exactly hold any weight or have any credence in the school. To quote the local parlance, they spoke pure pish. No, I'm not suggesting I was blameless. Not for one minute am I doing that. I'd admit that there was a part of me that enjoyed the attention, the ambiguity of the situation and, in a perverse way, the potentially dire consequences of the remarks being true. It's good to be noticed. After all, we are all narcissists at heart, are we not? I could have dined out on the tale in years to come.

To my recollection, Miss Croal and I never fully discussed the situation. There was nothing to discuss. Nothing. Our relationship continued in a similar vein. But that's not to say that it wasn't hanging in the air, it was; but we never addressed it. The elephant hovered. I carried on with the study classes and my time spent in her English class was as it was: unfulfilling, unremarkable and uninspiring. That didn't make her a bad person or a bad teacher for that matter. The problem could have been me. I understood she was pitching her lessons to a class that was inferior to my academic prowess. That's not snobbery or arrogance on my part, that's reality. I wasn't challenged. Thousands of students like their teachers, and vice versa.

The thing is sooner or later you'll be hunted. Sooner or later they'll sniff you out. In any environment, you get a sense of who to steer clear of. This new school was no different. They wandered around in packs. No less than four, no more than twelve. They looked malnourished and unkempt. What struck me was the state of their skin, it looked damaged and unhappy. The complexion of poverty. Two had distinctive scars straight down their right cheeks in what appeared to be a premeditated assault. To my innocent and naïve eye it did, anyway. These scars were worn like badges and sent out a

clear message of intent to onlookers. It worked, I was…
terrified would be the wrong word to use…perturbed would
be more accurate. I was perturbed by them, the scars that is.
On the rare occasion I heard them chatting among
themselves, I found it nigh on impossible to understand what
they were saying. The odd word here and there. Their tone
and temperament, on the other hand, was easier to decipher. I
stayed clear of them.

I tried to make myself invisible around them, to draw no
attention to myself. Did it work? No chance. As an English-
man in a Scottish school, I may as well have hung a red neon
sign on my back saying *English guy! Feel free to kick the shit out
of him.* At first it was stares and internal questioning: 'Who the
hell is that?' 'When did that prick come to our school?' And
they were not wrong about the use of *our*; it was their school,
too. They controlled it. They provided its foundations. They
controlled where other students wandered…as well as some
teachers. They controlled the atmosphere of each lesson. After
that came the odd bark, 'Haw fanny man, wit ir you doin up
here?' 'Git back tae yer own country, ya bawbag.'

Never once did I retaliate or make, what could have been,
a misinterpreted gesture. Usually I plugged my earphones in,
and blocked their comments out. As long as they remained
just comments I could handle it, no problem. Keep eyes on the
floor! Keep eyes on the floor! Keep eyes on the floor! My
mantra when they were about. What galled me most was that
these lowlife bastards drove fear into the vulnerable and
insecure. Sought out and preyed on the weak. I was
determined not to appear weak.

117

I was warned in advance by a few good souls in the school. People who obviously knew what they were capable of. I listened. I understood.

'See those NEDs, man?' Conor Duffy said.

'NEDs?' I asked.

'The mad squad, the wans wey the trackies oan an the greasy napper.'

'You mean funny mad, or mad mad?'

'Listen, Clem, me old son, the mad squad ir the only wans in this school tae watch oot fur.'

'Really?'

'A'm tellin ye.'

'So NEDs would be like chavs where I come from?'

'Dae these chavs carry?'

'Excuse me?'

'Knives, chibs, screwdrivers...dae they carry?'

'I suppose some of them do. My last school didn't really have a problem with chavs or NEDs.'

'Thir the same hing, then.'

'Like I said, we didn't have a problem with them.'

'Well this wan diz. We hiv a major problem wey NEDs,' Conor said. I sensed the anger in his voice as well as a little seduction. Or maybe it was the way his dialect, put on or not, danced around and escaped from the side of his mouth. There was a perceptible pride to it as well. Like the pride of attending a school that so happened to house the maddest guys in mad town. My feeling was that Conor would be dining out for many years to come on his stories of surviving a school riddled with a NEDs plague. Tales would be fabricated and stories of fraternising embellished. Who knows, perhaps he could put together some sort of survival manual in the future.

'Well, I'll stay clear of them,' I said.

'Dae that, ma man.'

'To be honest, I doubt I'll have any dealings with them, Conor.'

'Make sure ye don't coz these mental bastards would hiv nae qualms aboot chibbin an English guy like yersel.' Then came a theatrical pause. 'Nae qualms at aw.' He did a mock stabbing motion with an imaginary knife. (He was in the exam class for drama). That's how I learnt what chibbing was. The verb 'to chib.' I liked it. But I couldn't foresee a context of when I could, or would, use it.

'Okay. I'll keep that in mind.'

'Aw it takes is a wrang word or lookin at sumbudy the wrang way.'

'Thanks.'

'Seriously, man, tread carefully aroon those psychos.' Then Conor's little friend entered the conversation. A feeble-looking guy, who had a ton of goodness about him, and not much else by the state of his dishevelled clothes; he was affectionately referred to as Wee Sean.

119

'They need nae excuse, dude.' I sniggered at the use of the word dude, which triggered Wee Sean's I'm-as-serious-as-cancer persona into action. 'I'd advise you tae keep yer trap shut aroon those mental loons.'

'I intend to.'

'We're nae tryin to frighten ye ir anythin like that, it jist thit they might take exception tae yer accent.'

'Cheers.'

'Nae bother, dude,' Wee Sean said, evidently content with his role as security consultant. My face must have contorted into a symbol of worry.

'Don't panic, Clem, me old son,' Conor said, with an air of reassurance.

'No, I'm okay. Seriously.'

'Look, thir in the remdems anyway so ye won't hiv much tae dae wey them.'

'Remdems?' I asked.

'It means remedial.'

'What, all of them?'

'Ivry last wan, dude,' Wee Sean said.

'Listen, forget that, dae ye play fitbaw?' Conor asked me.

'I'm afraid I don't. Rugby was what we played at our last school.'

'Nae luck,' Wee Sean said.

My negative response hammered the death nail into the

conversation. That was me firmly out of the gang. Not that I wished to join it in the first place, but if I had any aspirations to be a part of it there was no chance. Above all else they probably thought I was gay. Not liking football has that effect on other males. It seems to be the main contributing factor to being homosexual. A prerequisite for entry into the gay set.

Lies

Rosie was fluctuating between being pissed off and making a half-arsed attempt at blanking me. She was fluctuating between talking and not talking. Her best friend, Cora, was giving me some serious intense looks as well. The evils as they say up here. At first I put it down to teenage girl things and then to girl things in general, and then, as it continued, I put it down to a Glasgow thing. The cold shoulder troubled me. Cora, I couldn't have cared less about, but Rosie troubled me. We had been getting on brilliantly. I was spending loads of time at her house teaching her the guitar, listening to tunes and generally chilling out.

She had a cool room. I loved just doing nothing with her, hanging out. I had never really experienced it like that before. We took our relationship to the next level in that room. We had become a damn good partnership. Solid. Both of us had almost mentioned the L word. That's why it was so confusing that she was demonstrating this kind of behaviour. By the Tuesday afternoon it had gone on too long. I raised the issue in our Italian class. Was there a chink that had somehow alluded me? A caveat?

'Have I done something?'

'What?'

'Have I done something wrong?'

'I dunno, have you?'

'That's what I'm asking, Rosie.'

'Well if you don't know, don't expect me to tell you.'

'Tell you what?'

'It's nothing.'

'It's obviously something, Rosie. You haven't broken breath to me for almost two days.'

'What are you going on about? Course I have.'

'Trust me, you haven't.'

'What are we doing now?' Rosie asked.

'You know what I mean.'

'Do I?'

'Look, stop being so mental, if you have something to say to me then spit it out. I can't be doing with all this evasive shit.'

'Don't start throwing your fancy words in my direction.'

'Jesus, never mind.'

'Rosie! Clem! Any problems?' Mrs Lenihan interrupted.

'No, Miss.'

'No, Miss.'

'Okay, good. Get on with it then.' And we did get on with it. Copying verb conjugations into our notebooks as if our lives depended on it. We were playing that game where the action engaged in was intensified while the mind was pin balling around a completely different subject matter.

'I wasn't not talking to you, by the way,' Rosie whispered.

'Well, what is it then?'

'Have you not heard the rumours?'

'What rumours?'

'What rumours? The rumours of you and that slapper Croal.'

'What?'

'You heard.'

'What's Cora been saying now?'

'Cora didn't say anything. She didn't need to,' Rosie barked.

'GET ON WITH IT YOU TWO!' Lenihan said.

'I'll speak to you after class,' I whispered.

If it wasn't cowering away from the school's nutters it was shielding myself from the rumour rousers and gossip-mongers. Not that I wish to go on and on about my old school, but in my old school it was perfectly natural, and somewhat encouraged, to establish and build relationships with teachers. If you applied a similar belief system in this environment it obviously meant you were either sucking someone's cock or trying to shag them. What sadness. What a fantasy world. Did these people exist in the vacuum of television soaps and juvenile junk mags? How utterly pre-posterous. I despised each and everyone of them for this slur. For trying to separate Rosie and me. A shambolic shower if ever there was one; I hated the way they all purported to be free of their adolescence, I loathed the way they flaunted their pathetic adult demeanour and I detested the way they presented their sordid zeitgeist philosophies to whoever would listen. This odious spawn of *Big Brother* and *X Factor* could be exposed with the click of a finger, yet here they were collectively spreading their vile lies about me. It's a bad place to be when the mind allows you to empathise with those mad bastards who shoot up their school somewhere in the US...or Germany. It's the daily humiliation they undoubtedly suffer at the hands of their victims, along with the isolation, that sends them over the edge. In some macabre sense, they themselves have been killed way before those who soon will be. That was as far as my empathy took me.

I left school early that day, directly after Italian class. I had no appetite for them. No stomach for any discussion with Rosie. In any case it would only have uprooted the anger I had of seeing her hunched behind a car outside the school's main entrance a few weeks previously. Spying. Badly. What happened was Miss Croal and I were chatting after the study class. A nondescript student-teacher chat – something about the future and what I wanted to do, where I saw myself in years to come; the same chat most teachers have with their senior students. I think it made them feel empowered and worldly by passing on their words of wisdom to us fledglings – pretty dreary really.

Here's the thing, halfway through the conversation I caught a glimpse of Rosie out the corner of my eye, wedged between two car bumpers. She was just staring at us, screwing her face up like people do when they are trying hard to hear. As if it makes a difference. Bonkers behaviour. My initial thought was to shield her from Miss Croal's gaze for fear that she would cause everyone concerned unnecessary embarrassment. Least of all me. I didn't want the conflict with Rosie

125

so I let it go. I wrapped up the conversation and rebuffed Miss Croal's offer of a lift. It was in everyone's best interests.

The biggest disappointment with our conversation in the Italian class and the car bumper incident was that I believed Rosie to be above all the bullshit and innuendo that went on at the school. It was one of her more attractive qualities. I was angry with her for sinking to the same level as her peers. For actually allowing herself to be complicit in the tittle-tattle, for questioning my integrity, for being utterly ridiculous.

After that untruthful bile spread like an Australian bush fire, I cut myself off from the others at school, which wasn't that difficult as friends could be counted on a hand with one finger, acquaintances on the other. Behind their looks a new narrative was being constructed, one beyond that of simple query and conjecture. In their minds each and every one of them had me sussed and, thus, tailored their chat, their stare, their silence accordingly. That was okay, for me what was worse was the laughter behind the hands. I couldn't seem to get to grips with that. Or the exaggerated sniggers when I passed them by. Usually it took about five paces for it to begin. The sound of it pierced through me. And it wasn't all about the cancerous lies either, it could have been about my hairstyle, my clothes, my shoes, the badges on my bag, the music I listened to (not that any of them would have known what I was listening to). The style of my headphones came under their scrutiny and chagrin also. Anything that took their fancy really.

Did I mention the ritual piss taking of my accent? I had to laugh myself at the poor imitation that some of them attempted to make. They couldn't quite master the pronunciation of my southern English accent, especially *ing* words. Some particular elevated dimwits screeched out Scouse and Cockney accents. I tried to baffle them by refusing to talk or participate in class. I basically shut up. It didn't work.

Warm hearted with a plentiful blend of black humour was what the book said about Glasgow. Obviously its researchers never ventured close to this place.

'I don't care what any of they dickheads say, Clem. It's just me and you against they bastards,' Rosie said.

'What about Cora?' I said.

'She's just a jealous wee bitch at times, don't mind her.'

'I don't, it's you I'm worried about.'

'I'm not the one getting pure pelters at school all the time.'

'I can handle it.'

'They're evil bastards,' she said.

'Don't worry. It'll be over soon.'

'If any of them say anything to my face, I'm telling you, I'll have them.'

'I wouldn't get too upset about it, if I were you.'

'Wee fuckin NED numpties. Especially that Fran McEvoy, I hate that prick.' Rosie said. I found this funny. A few months ago I wouldn't have had a clue what an expression like 'NED numpties' meant. But I did agree with her about McEvoy.

'Just leave it, Rosie.'

127

'Well, it affects me an all, you know.'

'I know, but let's just leave it.' We cuddled. 'Let's continue, shall we?' We kissed.

'But I'm pure shite at guitar.'

'It's okay, I'm a good teacher.'

Music

They came out of nowhere, and I mean nowhere. It wasn't as if there was an abundance of snow on the ground. You'd have been hard pushed to form a proper snowball from the stuff that remained.

I filled up my iPod with some winter music and skipped off to school. Usually I met Rosie on the way, but this morning she was off to an art gallery with the rest of her advanced higher art class. I was flying solo. Or so I thought.

Twenty yards from the school gate.

Swoosh!

These things were frozen solid like ice. As I said, I didn't see them.

Bang!

Back of the head, just behind the ear. Surge of pain. Hand goes to the hit zone, head turns to the direction of the thrower, my oppressor.

Swoosh!

Another missile in full flow, slow mo. Too late to duck.

Smack!

Direct hit in the eye socket.

Both hits demonstrating an accuracy and skill of a master marksman.

Compliments.

Bent double holding the eye, thinking the most horrid

thoughts. Snot escaping from my nose, something seeping out of my eye. Hopefully just the water from the ice ball. It feels neither hot nor cold, which leads me to believe it's blood. Or worse, a pus-like liquid. Danger juice. Don't take the hand away. Leave it on there, press tight on it, keep the eye in place, don't let the little bugger fall out. If you let it fall out you're done for.

Forever.

Hold it in place. Don't bother looking to see if it's blood or water, just concentrate on holding it in place. Don't concern yourself with the throbbing pain in your head either, the stinging and throbbing ear, the continuous ringing sound, the wet collar of your shirt.

Is it water or blood?

Hold that hand on the eye. Hold tight.

Don't let the little bugger fall out and roll away. It's not a ball, it won't bounce back to you. It won't bounce back into its home. Don't let it roll away down a drain or onto the bumper of a passing car.

Listen to the song and stay calm. I'm sure it's only water. *M. Ward* sings lovely songs. Soothing to the ear on a winter's morning. A touch of brightness to an otherwise dull day. Embrace it.

Sing it *M*.

It's hard to hear through one earphone with the ringing sound going through the other. Cars and voices and laughter as well.

Who's laughing? Who in their infinite wisdom is laughing at my misfortune?

Step forward; state your name, your aim.

This is the devil incarnate, the ice launcher himself. No sympathy for him. The creator of this mess can be heard out of my ringing ear. A compendium of noises now plays *M.Ward*, continual ringing and this wacko's voice.

Sneering. Sniggering. Snarling.

KEEP HOLDING THAT EYE. I told you.

'Howz yer eye?' Scum 1 asked.

'Ye need tae watch oot fur snowbawz roon here,' Scum 2.

'Aye, kood take yer eye oot way wan ay they things,' Scum 3.

Laughter. Lots of laughter. Waiting for the kick. Waiting for the punch. The finale. The dénouement. The crunch. The slap on the jaw. The head-butt to the temple. The knee to the ribs. Blood or water?

'Ya English cunt,' some other scum piped up.

'Up here stealin oor fuckin wimin,' another scum quips.

'Shaggin oor teechurs,' the final scum says.

Footsteps on the move. Then they're gone. Blood boiling. Let the good ear breathe.

Take out *M. Ward*, no need for a sprinkling of sunshine anymore. Revenge music is required. Hardcore stuff. Get yourself in the mood. Get yourself back to an upright position. Take deep breaths – in...out...in...out. In through nose…out through mouth… Take your time. Hand on eye. Hand shaking like a terrified leaf. A little leaf lost in a fairground.

Alone.

Hand hot from holding the eye in its house. Locking the door. Mind petrified to think about the consequences.

The revenge. Fearful of the reprisal. The reprisal of the monster with one eye and dodgy hearing.

He'll come. Disabled or not. He'll come.

Monsters can only take so much, you see. Keep knocking and the monster will come out. Hibernation is over. The dormant will soon dominate.

Can feel eye rising. Swelling. So big it's about to explode.

Like a boxer after going the distance.

My distance is away from the school gate.

Got to get home. Anywhere but here. Anywhere but here. Hand on eye. Hold tight.

Earphones dangling. Good ear pulsating. Head bursting. Sweat streaming. Good eye drowning. Blood boiling. Brain simmering. Got to remain calm, focus. Focus for the future. Who was laughing at me? Was Fran McEvoy laughing at me? Did he take aim? Did he lay in wait and take aim? Did he tightly fashion two balls of ice together, lay in wait and take aim? Did he tightly fashion two balls of ice together, lay in wait, take aim and launch the snowballs at my head?

Did that McEvoy engineer to cause me pain and

humiliation? Did he want to see me hurting? This goes beyond name calling, beyond pig-ignorant behaviour. Goes beyond what I'm capable of doing. Beyond what I want to do. Beyond what I imagine in my head, my poor head, of doing. Time to hand out my own form of punitive justice. Can't let the bastard get away with that. Taunts I can take. Two ice bullets and degradation I can't. Would be seen as impertinent to recoil from this, an invitation for more?

What next for the whipping boy? Got to show them I'm not afraid. Greater figures than me have made greater stances, taken greater strides. I shall not be perturbed.

Glasgow with its 'No Mean City' tag. Secretly proud of its tag. Wears the tag on its sleeve, on its collar, on its socks, on its arse. Surely No City Means to dish out this?

Glasgow, I didn't mean to step on your toes. I didn't mean to infiltrate. I didn't mean to steal yer wimin. I didn't mean to befriend yer teechurs. I didn't. I didn't.

Glasgow.

I didn't mean to be here.

Advice

'What in the fuck happened to your eye?' Rosie said, with a genuine sense of concern about her tone. The bruising and swelling instantaneously erased much of the awkwardness that had been in the air following the Miss Croal issue. My bad eye saved the day.

'It was nothing,' I said, just delighted to see her.

'Nothing my arse. It's pure swollen up.' She reached out to touch it; I flinched like they do in the movies. Very melodramatic indeed. I was playing the hero role: tortured, almost broken and self-pitying yet still alive and ready to fight another day. Did I mention handsome? (How handsome can one be with a shiner?)

'It looks much worse than it is.'

'Who hit you?'

'A snowball.'

'But there's no snow.'

'It was more like an iceball really.'

'Fuck.'

'That's what I said as well. Among other things.'

'I thought someone hooked you.'

'More honour if it had been.'

'Who did it?'

'I don't know.'

'My arse you don't know.'

'I don't.'

'Who are you trying to protect?' she said, once again trying to place her fingers on the swelling. Trying to take care of me. A show of affection, which I spurned. 'Let me see it.'

'It's nothing, seriously.' She sighed. I sighed. We stared at each other for longer than we should have. She was reading me. She could tell from my expression that I was being dishonest.

'Was it who I think it was?'

'I don't know. Who do you think it was?'

'That little NED prick McEvoy and his cronies?'

'Oh, I'd say you're warm.'

'What do mean warm? I'm roasting.'

'I'll give you hot.'

'I knew it was them.'

'How can you be so sure?'

'Half the school are talking about it.'

'Is nothing sacred in this place?'

'Are you kidding, that prick McEvoy'll be going around school acting like the dot bomb.'

'The dot what?'

'Like a fucking big shot.'

'It seems you already knew what had happened?' Then

there was another longish pause. I could see her mind was in concocting mood.

'We need to do something about it.'

'The swelling will go down in a few days, it looks worse than it is.'

'Fuck the eye, get some frozen peas. You'll see again.'

'We don't have any frozen peas.'

'Fuck the peas, stick your head in the freezer then.'

'What are you going on about?'

'I'm talking about Fran McEvoy.'

'What about him?'

'We have to do something.'

'No, we don't,' I said.

'He won't go away you know.'

'Guys like that always go away.'

'Yeah, tell me when?'

'Eventually.'

'Not this type.'

'What do you propose then, agent Scully?'

'What?'

'Oh, never mind…what's the plan?'

'We have two options. Either we do something and put a stop to all this shite once and for all or he'll just continue with what he's doing.'

'What's option number two?' I asked.

'Don't really know that yet.'

'Option number one I understand, I get it, but in reality what can I do?'

'How do I know?'

'You're the one who said we had two options.'

'Yeah, but I don't know what they are, do I?'

'Oh, okay, well thanks for shedding some light on proceedings for me.'

'All I'm saying is that if you don't do something about it, this is how it's going to be for you everyday at school,' she said, pointing to my eye. The affectionate gesturing had obviously evaporated. I didn't tell her about my pulsating ear or pounding headache.

'Do you think I'm not aware of that?'

'You have to challenge him, Clem.'

'What, to a duel?'

'You know what I mean.'

'What can I do? I'm alone here. I can't singlehandedly fight Fran McEvoy and his posse. Besides, it's not part of my composition.'

'You have me.'

'What?'

'You're not alone, you have me.'

'Are you telling me you moonlight as a vigilante now?'

'I protect what's close to me,' she said. Another pause, more like impasse. We hugged. We pecked. She gently kissed my eye. The pressure of her lips made me wince. Sore.

'We'll think of something,' I said.

'It has to be something drastic, coz I can't stand that bastard.'

'Maybe it's just about keeping a low profile.'

'What do you mean? Not going to school and all that?'

'No, but avoidance while I'm there would be a good start.'

'It won't work. He'll know what you're up to.'

'He could forget about the whole thing and move onto the next victim.'

'Don't you get it? You're prime meat because you don't come from around here. You're no threat to him, just fodder.'

'So what are you saying?' I asked.

'You need to get to him before he gets to you.'

'Attack him?'

'I'm saying give him some sort of message that will make him think twice about coming near you again.'

'I get that, but what?'

'Come on, you're a smart guy Clem, much smarter than that wee wanker any day.'

'Words won't hurt him, Rosie.'

138

'No, but some good old fashion sticks and stones might.'

'So you're saying I should beat him up with sticks and stones? Assault him with weapons? GBH stuff?'

'Believe me, he wouldn't think twice about using them on you.'

'What's wrong with you people up here?'

'And his little helpers wouldn't just stand back and watch either.'

'And what happens after I beat the living daylights out of him, assuming, that is, that I can, and leave him all battered and bruised? What happens after his convalescence period is over, eh? Where does that leave me?'

'I don't know.'

'I'll tell you, shall I? It leaves me in a much more precarious position than the one I find myself in right now. Not only that, but I'll be entering into the world of criminality, and I didn't come here to be a criminal. Jesus, I can't believe this, all I want to do is get my qualifications from that excuse of a school and get the hell out of here.'

'Hell out of here where?'

'South, I don't know, Brighton maybe.'

'And what about me?'

'Let's not have this conversation right now.'

'When do you propose we have it, then?'

'Another time, just not now.'

139

'Were you ever going to tell me what your plans were? Or were you just going to spring it on me one day?'

'You knew. I told you right at the start. You knew.'

'Yes, but I thought things might have changed a wee bit, given what we've been through together. The things we've experienced.'

'We're just going out with each other, Rosie, it's not as if we've travelled to the ends of the earth or anything like that,' I said. Silence, suddenly anger and hurt had popped in to say hello. 'And you could hardly call what we've been through an *experience*. Even the term *been through* is inaccurate to some extent. We haven't *been through* anything significant, Rosie. This is delusional thinking,' I said, with as much venom and dishonesty as my eye, ear and head would allow me to muster. I sensed the tears arriving. Shoulders shaking. Rage rising. A lethal cocktail, especially in Rosie.

'I lost my fuckin virginity to you.'

'What?'

'I let you fuck me.'

'How eloquent.'

'I gave you my body, Clem.'

'Are you looking for thanks?'

'An acknowledgement of it at least. It's a big deal, you know.'

'This is melodrama.'

'Don't dare stand there and insult me.'

'Look, I didn't come here to argue,' I said.

'I don't want to argue with you, Clem.'

'Me neither.'

'I thought you came here to thrash out a plan to relieve yourself from the clutches of McEvoy?'

'I did,' I said. She started crying. It was the first time I saw her crying. It disconcerted me. It doesn't happen that often but I relent whenever tears arrive. I once caught a glimpse of mum sobbing when news first broke of our move to Glasgow, it was a hard sob with breaks in her breathing and high-pitched yelps; subsequently I caused no hassle of my own, although I so badly wanted to demonstrate my teenage angst. I played my guitar instead.

What I said about Brighton wasn't meant. At least half of what I said wasn't meant. Try telling Rosie that. Nevertheless it had to be said at some point. What was the point of putting off the inevitable? I'd be lying if I said I wasn't troubled by her desire to see me inflict pain upon another human being; so maybe I was driven to trying to hurt her feelings.

I fully understood the McEvoy situation had to be dealt with, but it was weird as hell to have my girlfriend, whom I regarded as a neo-pacifist, inviting and almost prodding me into taking punitive action. Not an attractive trait. Was this part of the Glaswegian female's fabric? One who stands beside (or behind) her man while he dishes out reprisal and retribution? One who fights fire with fire? I don't fight fire with fire. Unless I'm being scorched to cinder. The only time I have raised my fists in rage was a thunderous smack on Matt

Seed's chin because of his obsession with the word faggot, which was constantly aimed in my direction. Thud! Never did I hear that word muttered towards me again. I felt terrible though. I mean, one punch can kill a man. I didn't want to be a one-punch killer.

'Look, I'm upset. I mean, look at the state of me.'

'I'm upset too.'

'I didn't mean to hurt you, Rosie,' I said. We embraced yet again. My eye still beating. My ear still ringing. My desire to remain in this city eroded. 'I'm just sick of this place at times. All the posturing. All this hard man shit. All the small men wanting to be big-time gangsters.'

'I know,' she said. I held her tight, feeling her tears wet against my shoulder. 'I hate it, Clem.'

'Me too.'

'We need to get out of this place.'

'We will.'

'Promise?'

'Promise,' I said, knowing full well it was a promise I could neither fulfil nor commit to. 'And don't worry about Fran McEvoy and his cronies.' Which sounded as though I would take care of that lot, which certainly wasn't the case.

'I'll try.'

'Promise?'

'Promise,' she said. I gave her a peck on the cheek, tasting her salty tears. I knew full well it was a promise *she* could neither fulfil nor commit to.

'Everything will work out,' I assured her.

'For the best?' she asked.

'For the best.'

'Come and we'll get that eye sorted out.'

Cheek

She succeeded in touching my eye. I didn't invite it, she just placed one finger on it and then stroked it gently with four fingers. My initial thoughts shifted to other people who may have been hovering around. For some reason I was fearful, acutely aware of where I was. I had been apprehensive on the walk to school but felt a strange sense of protectiveness when I entered the main doors. The corridors would act as a kind of safety buffer. But when Miss Croal put her hand on my eye my heart rate frightened me, I gulped my saliva much harder and I could hear a croak in my voice.

'Oh, Clem, what happened?'

'It was nothing Miss, I got hit with a snowball,' I croaked.

I felt ashamed. Undeveloped for her caress. I wanted to be in control, be a man, show the world, her, that I could handle any eventuality, any pitfall that came my way. I was invincible. That I was immune to puerile schoolboy behaviour. Now I was the walking embodiment of just this, with the bruising to match. Before, she viewed me as an equal, a contemporary, someone who could debate, discuss and divulge. Now she wanted to take care of me, as teachers are programmed to do...at times. She pitied me, playing the conscientious teacher in their pastoral care role. I was now just another schoolboy. Blended and branded.

'It looks very swollen, Clem.'

'It looks worse than it is.'

My rattling heart reaffirmed that I was what she thought I

was. Even though it was early in the morning I was petrified that one of Rosie's mates, Cora I mean, would saunter around the corner and misconstrue this as a physical display of affection. A crime. The end for both of us. Or worse, one of the NEDs would get an eyeful, put two and two together and come up with eighteen. Or worse still, McEvoy. In any case word would spread quicker than a prostitute with butter smeared thighs. Words like ILLICIT, ILLEGAL and SACK would be swirling around before morning break. Did this woman not know what she was doing? Was she unaware of the danger she was placing herself in? Was she so blatantly naïve?

'Is it sore to touch?'

'A little.'

The pain was much more intense than what any hand could have achieved. Her fingers never left my eye through-out this exchange, it seemed like time had become obstructed, all movement had slowed down to a funeral pace. I was terrified that we would be caught. Please take your hand away Miss. Miss, please take your hand away. I don't think you should be touching me. You are overstepping the boundaries. You're going to get caught. Take a step back from this woman. Take a step back from this man. This boy. Distance yourself from this crazy woman. My eyes flicked left. Right. Right again. Left. And back again. I was tran-scending discomfort. She could feel it, no doubt. She could feel it.

'Have you had it checked out?'

'No, it will be okay in a few days, or so.'

I could hear noise. She could hear noise. Voices in the distance. Approaching. An enquiry. A walking gaggle. A real-life fire alarm. Danger. Voices. Then her fingers left my eye. Not abruptly, but tentatively removing each finger one by one, touching my cheek in the process. Or did I just imagine that? Both of us each took a baby step back. The voices came closer. The fucks, wankers, fannies and bastards were perceptible now.

'Who did this to you?'

'I've no idea.'

'Come on, Clem.'

'Seriously Miss, I don't know.'

'Why would you protect those who did this?'

A mob of third-year boys passed by sniggering into their blazers and making furtive little comments. I heard the name Cora being mentioned more than once in a disparaging manner. My name also. If indeed *English Cunt* counts as a name. I heard Rosie's name, then McEvoy's. Their role model. Sniggers, giggling, laughter, hyperbolic comic hilarity. I was a laughing stock and these were just the third-years. There was more to come. A tsunami of abuse and mockery. Waves of danger.

'I honestly don't know who did it.'

'Was it that group of fifth- and sixth-year lads?'

'Who?'

'Nobody.'

'Conor Duffy?'

'No.'

'Then who?'

'Not Conor.'

'The lads who wear the tracksuits?'

I stared hard at the floor.

'Those NEDs?'

'Yes, the NEDs.'

A pause. A look. A stare. A glare. A tangible untruth in the air.

'No.'

'Clem, look, you know you can confide in me, if you feel unsafe.'

A hand. An extension. A recoiling. A reach. A retreat from those who teach.

'Thanks. I really appreciate that.'

A statement. A sentiment concaved. A bell. Ringing. Saved.

I think that was the last time myself and Miss Croal held a proper conversation. The shit and fan stuff happened soon after, smattering the metaphoric excrement on the faces of those in close proximity. The stench of it never to leave us: pervasive and intrusive. I'm not too sure what her take on it all was, nevertheless I'd be unhappy if she didn't vindicate me. That bell was the trouble that started it all. Well, that and a multitude of other things, and others. The bell rang, saving both of us. I made my way to maths. Shit subject, hard as hell. A safe haven…

McEvoy and a few of his lackeys were loitering about twenty yards from the door of the maths class. Nike, Burberry, cheap gold and wrist tattoos all exhibited. Wrist tattoos, the summation of life on the arm…in Cantonese, Arabic or Japanese. Instant inspiration at the flick of an eye. This crowd were an anomaly in this school, non-uniformed mavericks. They weren't waiting on anyone in particular. Surely not me. They certainly weren't waiting in an orderly fashion to enter no maths class either, basic counting maybe.

More sniggering at the bruise. McEvoy said something, which I couldn't penetrate beyond a growling grunt. The others laughed. Not wanting to look sullen, frightened or sad, I smiled. This sent him into an internal tailspin. His next action disturbed me and sent me into a similar spin of my own. He took his index finger and slowly dragged it from the top of his cheek to the bottom. Meticulously. Then the same stroke on the other cheek. All the time his eyes never once deviating from mine. It was a shuddering threat. A clear message of intent.

The lackeys laughed while my expression had irrepressibly changed. As long as it wasn't fear. Show them no fear. Dogs smell it. Don't allow them to smell it, not even the slightest whiff. Give them your *you'll-not-fucking-intimidate-me* gaze. Face your demons boy, I kept telling myself. McEvoy, the devil incarnate, indicating that he was going to draw a Stanley Knife, or something equally as sharp and accurate, from one part of my cheek to the other. Stating that he wanted to slash me, cut me open, slice a new smile onto me, disfigure me, destroy me. This repulsive piece of shit seriously wanted to leave his mark on me. Fran McEvoy's signature embedded on me for life. For life! I wouldn't get a job. Every ounce of existence would start to corrode and crumble beneath me. A rapid road to the gutter. In the depths of my despair I'd be able to chart it back to that pivotal moment outside the maths class. That moment I did nothing about it. Death by capitulation.

In silence, fear and anger I entered the class knowing that I had to get the hell out of that school. That same day. Directly after the maths class. Before the class. Shove the maths class. What was the point of concentrating on maths when the very fabric of my life was at risk? I sat down at that desk and wondered if I was being too histrionic. Just as I had reconciled myself with the fact that I was, McEvoy placed his head around the door and growled something at me before gesturing, once again, the self-same slashing motion. Then abruptly vanished.

'You want to watch him,' said a voice behind.

'Aye, he's a mad bastard,' said another.

I gave it a further five minutes, waiting for the corridors to become weary. For the racket to fade.

'Sir, can I go to the toilet, please?'

'Don't be long.'

I flipped my bag on my back, left the class, walked out of the school and vowed never to return.

That was the plan in any case.

Mobile

My heart vibrated. An incessant irritation in my chest.

Buzz, buzz, buzzing.

Like a queen bee on heat. Six calls from Rosie. Each one ignored. About fifteen text messages.

Ping! Ping! Ping!

Each one read, each one internalised, each one ignored. I should have probably switched it off but the attention was what I was holding on to. Feeling desired.

Buzz! Buzz! Buzz!

Don't Answer.

Ping! Ping! Ping!

Wer R U?

I am just about to get off an overcrowded bus, which stinks of stale fags and booze. The unemployed, the disenfranchised, the socially diseased we are all here. *Bonnie Prince Billy* sings in my ears and I feel every pang of the man's gut wrenching prose. Today is for suffrage and self-pity.

Ping! Ping! Ping!

CLEM, WER R U?

I am now flicking through the CDs in HMV. My mother will be ever so pleased. I am suffering the pedantry prose of *Madonna's* newest creation. The death of music. And to think those poor Malian kids will have to miss out on their indigenous music for this tripe. It's a shame. God love them. Only here because it's freezing outside. Glasgow winters attack without mercy; they show no respect to age, health, wealth or emotional turmoil.

Buzz! Buzz! Buzz!

Don't Answer.

Ping! Ping! Ping!

R U comin bak 2 skool 2day?

Not even a pack of rabid Rottweilers could drive me back into that place. My secondary education has ceased…as of today. Say my goodbyes to those who will miss me, it should take you about thirty seconds or so.

Ping! Ping! Ping!

Wer the FUK R U?

I am here. In this city. This Godforsaken place. The place where the wind would slice open your head and people would slice open your face. I am here. This is where I am. Not through choice, want or desire but somehow I find myself here.

Ping! Ping! Ping!

Hav I dun s'thing?

Join the queue. Each and every member of it has been guilty of doing something. The question is what have I done? Why does no one ask me that? But I understand the need for the question.

Buzz! Buzz! Buzz!

Don't Answer.

Ping! Ping! Ping!

Y R U Ignoring me?

Because it's the only power I have left. The only thing I have control over. Silence and anonymity. I am ignoring myself. No one knows me here. Now, no one has any demands over me or wants to do anything to me, apart from the sales assistants who want to part my money from me.

Ping! Ping! Ping!

Wots rong?

Well, apart from the fact that some little ignorant, delinquent fucker threatened to disfigure me (for life) for the crime of…God knows what, and I am terrified to confront it head on – coupled with the impending uncertainty of the future – not much is wrong with me. A grey cloud has followed us up here. My father is working at a job even his son thinks is shit and beneath him, how degrading and shameful that must be? I'd hate to imagine. My mother is like another woman; gone is the cheeriness and blind optimism of everything crap. But with regards to your question, everything is just fine and dandy.

Buzz! Buzz! Buzz!

Don't Answer.

Ping! Ping! Ping!

Wot hav I dun?

Rosie, you have been yourself. ROSIE. The architect of all this, all this evil. You made me fall for you. Crave you. Desire you. You made me believe in my own narcissistic nonsense:

the tortured guy, the music lover, the intellectual, the bookworm, the loner, the mysterious one, the introverted, the self-contained, the handsome and the self-assured. I believed in it all. You wanted all this so I provided it for you. All bullshit. Everything. Now I am being attacked and chided for this fraud.

Ping! Ping! Ping!

Clem...

I hate that damn name. That middle class identity. A name that has brought me nothing but isolation and insult since I can remember. A name that can't even be abbreviated. A malicious, moronic moniker. A name that has led to this. I place it all squarely at the feet of this name. It all starts with furtive little comments; then ridicule, then malevolence, then some bastard tries to impress some other bastards and, before you know it, that same bastard, or one of the other bastards, wants to leave a mangled mark on you. Clem.

Ping! Ping! Ping!

Did s'thing hap at skool?

Did something happen at school? Of course something happened at school! Why the need to ask? I have no friends up here, have I? School is the only place where I indulge myself in the chat of others, if permitted that is. You'd hardly find me wandering the streets with a gaggle of mates now, would you? That school has no harmony with individualism, you are not allowed to be different, or NOT like football. Or NOT have bigoted tendencies. It's like Chinese Communism in action.

154

Buzz! Buzz! Buzz!

Don't Answer.

Ping! Ping! Ping!

Pik up ur fon!

I don't want you to hear my voice crackle with anger and interpret it as an emotional defeat. That I was close to tears. That you 'could hear it in my voice.' You'd tell Cora how you could almost feel the wetness of my cheeks. How you could taste the salt. The simple reason is that I don't want to talk. Today is not a talking day, it's a day for solace and reflection.

Ping! Ping! Ping!

Stop being an arsehole!!!

You are such a shower of offensive oafs up here. What gives you lot the right to comment on everything with a barrage of expletives? Or rebut with insulting invectives? It demonstrates a lack of vocabulary and an inability of expression. A less than appealing Glaswegian affectation. I think in this context though arsehole is an inappropriate word to use.

Ping! Ping! Ping!

I heard about McEvoy...Cunt!

Who's a cunt? McEvoy or myself? Me or him? Clem or Fran? This is ambiguous, Rosie. Notwithstanding, it's an effective and appropriate use of the curse. Possibly the strongest and most powerful in the English language. The word that brings about the most amount of disapproving gasps from people. Using that word can, in an instance, turn

155

someone horribly against you.

I have often thought about that McEvoy cunt and tried to rationalise his actions, tried to look at it from his point of reference. To see things through similar eyes, to endeavour to understand: to see through those very eyes that tell me he is afraid of his future, of imminent unemployment, of leaving the security of school after fourteen years, of departing days that have been full of structure (and guidance), of having somewhere significant to go everyday, of getting to leave his unhappy home without being press ganged into 'finding a job.'

I have tried to understand his frustration because those around him wear the latest high street fashions, go on foreign holidays, discuss their futures, have lasting relationships; jealous because his family couldn't afford to buy him anything, to treat him or his siblings to any of the trappings his peers receive, sad because Fran's parents blame their own children for taking away their own youthfulness and stripping them of any happiness they themselves could have garnered from life. Consequently these parents have rejected and neglected poor Fran. They have chosen to settle for a life of poverty and state handouts. Maybe it's more simplified than that, he could have one of those abbreviated illnesses: OCD or ADHD or ODD or CUNT. Maybe he has autism, Asperger's syndrome or some other form of cognitive chaos that has yet to be discovered and/or diagnosed. Maybe he just forgets to take his Ritalin on a daily basis. I have looked through these eyes and tried to examine why he does what he does, why he says what he says, why he carries a knife on him at all times, but no matter how hard and for how long I look the answer is always the same: McEvoy is a cunt. A first class, top of the range fucking cunting cunt.

Or maybe he just needs a hug.

Buzz! Buzz! Buzz!

Don't Answer.

Ping! Ping! Ping!

Luv U!!

Ah, Jesus, Rosie you are pulling out all the stops now. This has never been discussed between us, at least without any level of seriousness behind it; it's an off-limits subject. I think this is a reaction to me saying I wanted to go to Brighton, isn't it? This isn't real love. It can't be. Can't you see this for what it is? Think about it, you'll be able to regale friends at university, at work, in the future, your husband and your children of your first big crush...or love, if you want to call it that. Look around and see all the lives that have been destroyed by these waves of first loves, the multitudes who have become trapped because of these first loves. The ones who'll have crooked necks from years of looking back, who'll have crooked minds with what they find there: regret and wonder.

Ping! Ping! Ping!

No mor credit...U no wer I am.

That is the problem with society; no one has any credit, or is given any credit. Peers give no credit to endeavour or merit. They berate you at every turn. So don't worry, Rosie, none of us has any credit. It's not a thing you excel in up here. Perhaps

I am being too harsh, not conciliatory enough, but stuff it, stuff it all.

The buzzing and pings stopped. I was still in HMV leafing through CDs that I had no interest in either buying or probing. It was the mechanics, the routine of doing something, being valuable, feeling that I belonged, that kept the fingers flicking. I missed the correspondence from Rosie. I missed the attention. We all need it.

Shopping

Wandering the streets was a bit like living in a new reality. For the first time I got to see a different side to Glasgow. I examined the people closely. I trailed some of them as they started their day, following them as they entered their places of work looking as though they were carting around the world's woes on their shoulders.

I played games with many of them throughout the day, detective games, discovered where many of them go for lunch, listening into their conversations: I was sitting in a bookshop café drinking their expensive, bucket-sized coffee, trying to decipher *B.S. Johnson's* words but the rambling fool who was sitting to my left and some scatty girls, who were sitting to my right, wouldn't allow me this basic pleasure. The fool was cracking on to a female friend (?) about some 'science research project' and 'future employment projections' of such a thing. The friend meanwhile appeared wholeheartedly disinterested. I found myself eavesdropping. Remarkably interested. I thought to myself: I wonder if they are sleeping with each other? They touched hands. They probably are, I surmised. Then I thought: if I were that woman I'd definitely not go with the science guy. Too humdrum. I'd shag the woman though (only once however, I couldn't put up with her vacant look for too long). Perhaps she digs the sedate scientist types I wagered. I then shifted focus to the scatty girls. I thought: I wonder if they're sleeping with guys yet? etc. etc. These people brightened up the dreary streets of Glasgow for me.

Then I simply got bored. I had exhausted my iPod player,

and got fed up with the selection. My finger was permanently pressed on the fast-forward button. I could listen to ten songs in five minutes with this counter-productive method. In the main I only kept them plugged into my ears to ward off unwanted interlopers, namely those young funky freaks who work in retail. Their enthusiasm being infectiously annoying and all that. All this 'how are you today?' crap. These homogenous, minimum wagers have mastered the blatantly obvious too. I mean, I'm in a shop, browsing rails and rails of overpriced clone clothes and out of the corner of my eye one of the groovy gang is hovering behind me resplendent with their spiky hair, skinny jeans, and a *Ramones* t-shirt asking me if I'm 'out shopping today?' Then next comes the killer tag for me, 'Do you need a hand with anything?' How difficult can it be to look at clothes? It doesn't take any effort that would require assistance. I am sure of that.

'Yes, in fact, I do need some help. Could you shift my eyes three millimetres to the left for me please?'

'No problem.'

'And could you adjust my feet for me as well?'

'Not a problem.'

'And what's this I'm looking at'?

'Well, that would be a t-shirt.'

'A t-shirt? And what do you do with that, then?'

IDIOTS.

I'm not sure if this is purely a Glaswegian trait or a retail pandemic.

It took me two full days of trawling the streets to come to my senses. Well, actually, it was after visiting the art supply shop that made me realise how utterly ridiculous I was being. A few weeks previously Rosie had brought me to the same art supply shop. I helped her buy some oil paints, some small canvasses, a Miró calendar and a scalpel knife. My helpful input was in fact the calendar. I remember being happy with Rosie at that time; we had gone there as part of Rosie's tour of Glasgow, the official tour that had been promised to me for weeks. In exchange for guitar lessons. After the art store she showed me the wonderful art gallery, which sat beneath the imposing university. Big brother watching over his younger sibling, it was a magnificent sight. Both trying to outdo each other for dominance and beauty. One an architectural delight, the other a Gothic monolith. I think she was secretly hoping that their aura would seep into my pores and, the university at least, entice me into its seat of learning. We zigzagged in and out of the student body and felt strangely grown up among them.

Then she took me to a fantastically cheap music shop. Classic *Bowie, Waits* and *Dylan* for a fiver. *Northern Soul: Dance Floor Fillers* for three quid. *Bukowski* and *Beckett* books for two quid. I was in my heaven. She showed me how to get there from where I was living. A short bus ride and then hop on Glasgow's quaint circular underground system. Easy. After searching for bargains we rode our luck by trying to get served in a little Irish pub that had pictures of their country's most famous scribblers all over the walls. We succeeded in our quest for two creamy pints of Guinness. Both of us huddling in the corner delighted with ourselves, unable to tell each other that the Guinness was a bit like drinking rancid tar. This didn't deter us, we bought another two. Each.

The darkness had set in as we again walked past the art gallery and university on our way back to the less salubrious part of town. Our hands tightly clasped, our gait slightly askew, our voices loud and cheerful; our drinking binge made us a touch tipsy. Their red and yellow lights illuminated the sky above us, both standing majestically, alongside our own inebriated majesty. I couldn't decide which one I liked best. I think the university because it was so daunting and significant, however, saying that, the gallery had a stately aroma about it that drew you in. In any case it was the most romantic day I had had in my hitherto youthful life. That day a part of me was thinking that we were this perfect match; that we'd be together for a long long time to come. Marriage, kids, the works. That we were this team stuck inside our very own impenetrable bubble. Whereas another part of me was thinking while I'd remember this moment forever I'd be able to dazzle future girlfriends with my knowledge of the city on trips to Glasgow, regaling them with tales of my time spent here. Like me they'd feel the gooeyness of the moment. We made love for the first time that night.

My phone had been switched off for the best part of two days. I knew that it would be full of missed calls and texts from Rosie when I gave it life again. Over my lost two days (very John Lennon) I had run over a multitude of permu-tations in my mind. A series of *what would happen if?* questions arose. Too many questions and not enough answers. Not any answers. One thing I was certain about was that I would have to return to school. I needed those exams, if nothing else, to get me the hell out of this place. I couldn't allow McEvoy to hamper my dreams. I was determined to succeed in life even if that meant being accompanied by a ten-inch scar. Talent would prevail. I mulled over a number of choices I had at my disposal:

1. Tell a teacher. (The bullied are told from an early age to tell a teacher if they are systematically confronted by the class knob. While this appears to have had an enormous amount of success at primary school level, in my case we were not dealing with the odd name-calling, shove in the classroom, tugging of hair or infantile reduction of character. And, anyway, I couldn't tell a teacher because all the teachers were intimidated as well. The self-preservation society wanted to protect their cars and classroom harmony).

2. Tell a parent. (Great idea if the parents in question had a modicum of influence in the school or could harness enough support to make a difference. Great idea if the parents could expel the right amount of intimidation to the scum at hand. Great idea if the victimised had parents who actually gave a toss about their offspring's education and well-being. Great idea if the parents protected their progeny proficiently enough against pernicious pricks. Great idea if the parents didn't appear apathetic to all things their descendants said and did, such as smoke dope in their bedroom and trawl the internet for free porn sites).

3. Seek restorative justice. (Under controlled circumstances converse with the tormentor and ask him/her why they undertook the action(s) they did; try to understand it from their point of view, be empathetic and compassionate. In essence it could prove to be a cathartic experience for all concerned. After a round of weak tea and cheap biscuits and a game of therapeutic tennis everyone would concur with the findings that there were, in fact, two victims in all of this. How content the assemblage will be in the knowledge that everyone is suffering. Ground-breaking work. They'll conclude that everyone has to take responsibility for their own actions, that those involved are to share the blame; even the maltreated innocents, who have regularly had the daylights kicked out of them, are culpable. Liberal bullshit, which only functions in exonerating the tyrant. Restorative justice? No thanks).

4. Confront the scum. (A distinct possibility that could go one of both ways. Anyone of a nervous disposition shouldn't be privy to any potential conversation/ confrontation. A gamble on a grand scale. Although perhaps the scum will respect the balls (or bawz) of the prey and show them the hand of deference. It would be a bit like a submission on the scum's part. A scum capitulation. Joy. Victory. A stay of execution. Nevertheless it could lead to a swift kick in the balls (or bawz) due to the scum's perceived understanding that insolence has taken place. A direct threat to his alpha male status. There were no two ways about it, it was a tricky situation).

Having spent two days emotionally malnourished, it was time to get my plate full again. School was beckoning. So was confronting Fran McEvoy.

Scum.

Plans

It was as if there was a troupe of trampolinists taking turns to do somersaults on my stomach. After pounding the streets of Glasgow all day I found myself lying on my bed, in the foetal position, listening to some of my mum's country albums and the battering rain outside. I don't know which was making me feel worse: the stomach pains, the weather or the pained voices in the music. All those break-ups, affairs, domestic violence and cash-flow problems. I was lying there thinking, bloody hell, why did we have to come to this shit excuse of a city, with its village mentality? (Rich, I know, coming from a boy from Eastbourne). I didn't have the energy to get up and turn the music off. I lay there and felt sorry for myself. It was an hour before I was due to be at Rosie's. I liked being punctual. A great virtue of mine.

'Come in, I'll get you a towel,' she said. Usually we kissed or did something affectionate, but it was evident that Rosie wasn't going to make that move. I didn't approach either, which made me think that I was the one who always instigated the kisses, hugs, holding hands, stroking hair and all that other touching stuff. I guess this time I just stood there like a wet blanket. It's funny when things are decided, you see people in a different light. Gone was all the *mysterious guy tag* that had been placed on me. For *mysterious* read *pathetic drip*. 'Don't just stand there, come in.' She handed me the towel.

'Thanks,' I said.

'Have you been out all day?'

'Yes.'

'Glasgow?'

'Yes.'

'Where did you go?' she asked.

'To the centre of the city and then the West End. Then I wandered around the university area and the grounds of the art gallery.'

'Sounds great.'

'It was okay, I suppose.'

'So that's what you did the whole day?'

'Pretty much.'

'Until now?'

'Yes.'

'Just walking?' she asked.

'And thinking.'

'It's a wonder you didn't get arrested.'

'I needed to think.'

'What about?'

'Us, school, Glasgow, me, you. Lots of shit. Pertinent shit.'

'Wow, sounds like a great day out.'

'It's what I needed to do.'

'I heard what happened at school.'

'Yeah, the guy's a mental case.'

'Head banger.'

'I'm going back tomorrow, you know.'

'Is that wise?'

'I can't run away forever, Rosie. I have to confront this guy…I have to.'

'I think I agree.'

'You do?'

'Yes. Confront the mentalist.'

'That's what I aim to do. I'm not going to allow this guy to intimidate me much longer. He's ruining everything.'

'Any ideas how you're going to handle it?'

'I have some idea, but I'm not adverse to seeking solace in some of the teachers or the police, if it comes to that.'

'I don't think it'll come to that.'

'I'm thinking of getting him on his own.'

'And then what?'

'Presenting him with a choice.'

'Of what?'

'Rationale or conflict.'

'Speak English, Clem,' she said. She said that a lot.

'I'm going to try and reason with him, and if he throws that back in my face then I will have no alternative other than challenge him to a scrap.'

'A square go? You are going to ask Fran McEvoy for a square go?'

'Just him and I.'

'Really?'

'With none of his merry band present. Just the two of us.'

'Clem…'

'…What other choice do I have?'

'None, I suppose.'

'Exactly.'

'But McEvoy is always fighting, like he has loads of experience in it. It's the one thing he's actually good at.'

'I played rugby at my last school.'

'Rugby! Big wow!'

'I'm stronger than him, and fitter.'

'I don't doubt it.'

'I fancy my chances if it's only the two of us, and fair.'

'With that maddo? He wouldn't know the meaning of fair.'

'Well if he's carrying anything I just have to be ready to deal with it.'

'Christ Clem, you sound as if you're excited by it.'

'I'm psychologically prepared.'

'And what if he doesn't take up the challenge? Then what?'

'Then I'll have to initiate it myself, won't I?'

'I think you should just stick to the first plan.'

'Of asking him to see sense?'

'Yes.'

'Just stick to that plan and I think you'll be okay.'

'You think?'

'I have a good feeling about it, let's put it that way.'

'Well let's hope it's the right feeling.'

'You don't want to do anything stupid.'

'I won't.'

'I know you Clem, you might do something impulsive.'

'I've played it out over and over in my head. I just need to stick to the plan.'

'Well, I'll support you.'

'Thanks,' I said. I was surprised at her support.

My plan for McEvoy was flawed. Flawed on so many levels. I needed one for Rosie and me. A plan that would say 'Rosie, it's been a blast old girl, but it's time to move on. I'll send you a postcard from Brighton.'

'It's late, Clem.'

'Yes, I should go.' I almost sprinted to the door.

'Okay, see you tomorrow, then?'

'Okay.'

'You'll be fine Clem. Try not to worry.' She placed her hand on mine. That's the type she was. I was different.

'I'll try.'

'I don't want you to get hurt.'

'I know you don't. We should protect each other,' I said. I think she thought I meant that I wanted her to protect me, but you could never tell with Rosie. She was being ambiguous again. She liked that word. I'd miss her. Really I would. I'd miss all the new words she enjoyed saying.

'We will.'

'Shall I pop round before school?'

'Erm…'

'…We can walk together.'

'If you like.'

'Okay, see you tomorrow, Rosie,' I said and pecked her on the cheek.

'Don't be late.' What was she saying? Of course I wouldn't have been late.

'I won't. Promise.'

'Night, then.'

'Night.'

She shut the door before I looked away. The curtains were being drawn as I reached the bottom of the path. It was curtains.

Smokers

There was something all too familiar with that morning's conversation. As though the previous night never existed. A peculiar déjà vu.

'I don't want you to get hurt,' Rosie said.

'I know you don't,' I said, 'I just got scared.'

'We should protect each other.'

'We will.'

When she went to gather her stuff for school I stood in reflective mood, weighing up the possible eventualities that would unfold. Feeling apprehensive, edgy yet strangely confident I was happy Rosie and I had discussed everything and she was standing beside as we went to school. My rock. The little devil on my shoulder, however, had different ideas and was nibbling at my ear quipping, *'just using this poor girl for your own means, there is no substance behind anything you say.'* While waiting at the doorway for Rosie to come bounding down the stairs, guilt penetrated my mind. I despised myself.

'Are you ready?' I shouted.

'A minute, just looking for something.'

'We're going to be late.'

'Why are you so eager?' she said as she scuttled down the stairs.

It was a still day, and still freezing. Both of us made breath circles from the cool air. Rosie blew bigger and more defined ones. Mine were whimsical and imperceptible. Rosie, I felt, could sense my anxiety, she broke long periods of silence with humorously inane conversations, which served only to try taking my mind off the proceedings.

'What would you call your band if you were in one?'

'I don't know.'

'Yes, you do, everyone has played that game. Come on what is it?'

'It's *Approaches to Learning*,' I said. Rosie guffawed and dismissed it out of sight.

'That's pure shite.'

'Okay, smart arse, what's yours?'

'Don't know, never really thought about it.' I liked that acerbic wit about Rosie.

'Don't talk shit, come on, I told you mine,' I said.

'Okay, promise not to laugh?'

'Cross my heart.'

'Okay, it's *Bedroom Busker*.' I held it for a moment giving the impression that I was mulling over the beauty of the band's name, my eyes tightening to suggest that I believed this was an inspired choice.

'Utter shit,' I said, but in truth I actually quite liked it.

'What?'

'I'd never buy anything from a band with a name like that.'

'You haven't a clue.'

This was followed by another long period of silence, not an

uncomfortable silence, but a type of silence that led me to think that Rosie was being overtly introspective and ponderous. Apart from my own predicament, there was something significant on her mind. Something more pressing than what was on my own, which then went haywire. Approaching the school I was thinking that this whole episode was all some big Glaswegian conspiracy against me. I envisaged turning a corner to discover McEvoy, the NEDs, Cora, Connor, Miss Croal and Rosie's mum all laying in wait. Coshes and clubs at the ready for their veritable feast. A lynch mob.

The red sandstone façade faced both of us. School. Not a soul to be seen other than eager first- and second-years. We hurried in. Rosie accompanied me to my first class, music, like some muscle bound bodyguard. We sat alone in the class plucking away at one of the guitars. I played her Pale Blue Eyes by *The Velvet Underground*, and told her it reminded me of her. A lie. She seemed impressed by this more than the tune. The bell rang. We embraced warmly before Rosie trudged off to her art class.

'I'll see you in English.'

'Okay.'

'Or do you want me to come and get you first?'

'No, it's alright. I'll be fine.'

'What if you bump into him?'

'We'll stick with the plan.'

The class was a nice distraction. Writing chord progressions for two periods and trying not to sound different from everyone else out there. As much as I tried to be original, it all sounded derivative and teenage. I'd never make it out of the confines of my bedroom. I was destined to be a bedroom busker forever. The bell rang and my heart started like a sprinter off the blocks. I waited back in the pretence of tidying up, labouring over putting guitars in their covers, plectrums in their box and music sheets in their folder. I even started to put the chairs under desks until the teacher got wind of my actions.

'That's fine, Clem, you're going to be late for your next class.'

'Yes.'

'Thanks. See you tomorrow.'

I hoped so. I really did hope so.

I walked briskly to English. Miss Croal looked happy to see me when I hurried into the class. The others already had their heads buried into some reading material. *Waiting for Godot.* I didn't have the heart to inform them that he never arrives. They were either going to be engrossed or dumbfounded by it. Rosie's eyes were planted firmly on me, relieved, no doubt, that I had made it safely between classes. She gave me a little wink. A very affectionate wink. Cora Kelly, who was sitting beside Rosie, made a joke face that suggested I was in some kind of trouble.

'Sorry I'm late, Miss.'

'That's okay,' she said, rather sycophantically. 'I see your eye is a little better.' Indeed my eye was much better, just a touch of yellow discolouring underneath the socket, but no swelling. Certainly all the wandering around in the cold for the past two days helped it recover.

'Yes, it was nothing really.'

'Like you said.'

'We've just started reading Beckett's *Waiting for Godot*,' she said, handing me a copy of the play. 'You are familiar with it, aren't you?'

'We read it at our last school,' I said.

'Aye right.' The voice from behind me spluttered. Cora Kelly.

'Some of us are just reading the intro.,' Miss Croal said. I took the book from her and made my way to my seat, opened the play at the introduction and began reading. It was familiar territory. Man's place in society. The meaning of existence. Why are we here? Why do we do the things we do? And then do them all over again? Beckett captured it and articulated it in an artistic, condensed fashion. I merely whispered, 'what the fuck...' when I needed answers to the bigger questions. There will come a time when I'll give up and not search for a response. This school was one of them.

The two periods flew by. As time generally does when you never want it to. Time plays games with you. The big hand hits you hard. When you need it to slow down it speeds up, and when you need it to run it toils. I pretended to read more Beckett, words flashing through the brain without meaning or reason. I was miles away. It sounded like a knelling bell. Rosie waited at the door for me. Cora hovered around as she could sense something wasn't quite right.

'Comin to the smokers?' she asked Rosie. Rosie looked at me as though waiting for my approval, which I gave with the flick of an eye.

'I'll see you back in here in ten,' she said. Cora had already made her way to get her nicotine fix. 'Clem, I'll stay if you want.'

'No, no. You go. It'll be okay. I'll just go down to the music room and fiddle about.'

'If you see him, just walk the other way.'

'What about the plan?'

'You won't have time, we only have about eight minutes now.'

'Okay, you better go. I'll see you back in here.'

Around every corner, every bend, every nook and cranny of the school building was the expectancy of McEvoy and his cohorts appearing. Lying in wait. Ready to ambush. Prepared to pounce. Walking towards the music room I chuckled to myself because the irony of the two lads waiting for Godot was not lost on me. Only their wait was full of anticipation, confusion and excitement in the main, while mine was full of apprehension and dread. All characters in this story waiting. One set in hopelessness the other one in expectancy. A significant difference was that my Godot would be sure to arrive. Maybe I was McEvoy's Godot? Was he waiting or searching? Searching for Clem! Doesn't seem to have the same ring to it. Searching for Clem! No.

Each scream, cry or chant was amplified. Every time I heard a noise from behind me my heart boxed my chest and my ribs juddered. I was just waiting for the next sound to be the determinant one: 'Haw! You, ya English fanny.' 'Wit did a tell you aboot cumin back in this school?' Perhaps it would have been much better to have the physical attack from the outset, without warning, to avoid any unnecessary vocal confrontation. A couple of punches to the back of the head, a few hard digs in the kidneys, an array of boots into the stomach. (I'd tense it up for them). A swift stampede. Much better to have it done inside the school, my thinking being this way it would only last a few seconds before someone would inevitably come to my aid, a conscientious member of staff. A true professional. Integrity. Anything happening outside school could be a relentless free for all. In my experience I have realised that the teachers here tend not to want to get their hands dirty at any shenanigans taking place outside the school gates. Outside their jurisdiction. Outside their school. I was safe in and around those corridors.

I made it to the music room in one piece. Some of the emo and grungier kids had made it there before me and had nabbed the best guitars. Trying to play some *Green Day* power chords, or some other band of similar ilk. I liked these types of students. Generally they were friendly, inoffensive and well into their music, as well as their image. They looked like ghouls with the remnants of the previous night's eye-liner, exhausted faces from their play station exertions and arms filled with silver and leather accessories. They spoke a weird hybrid of Glaswegian and pseudo-American slacker dialect. Throwing around phrases like 'Check this cool wee tune out, dude.' I found it amusing. I enjoyed being around these dudes in the music room. Before I could play an A D E7 A progression trying to capture the beauty of Dylan's *Visions of Johanna* the bell had already gone. I sang the first line to myself. I thought about replacing Johanna with Rosie, but there was syllable concern. Back to English. Back to waiting.

Once again I arrived late into class. A waft of stale smoke permeated around the room smacking me right in the face as soon as I entered. Did everyone in the class head direct for the smokers at interval? Did anyone abstain? My tardiness, for the second time in just over an hour, didn't go down too well with Miss Croal.

'This is the second time during this class, Clem.'

'Sorry Miss, I got held up in the music room.'

'Well, once is a mistake, twice is taking the proverbial.'

'It won't happen again, Miss.'

'Well, it's not good enough,' she said, as though scolding a child. I didn't quite know how to react. I stood in silence looking at her. 'Oh, just take your seat.'

I think she was trying to prove a point to the rest of the class. Exerting her authority. Demonstrating how she treats each pupil equally. No pets. No favourites. No crushes. Trying to quash rumours. Trying to get the girls onside. Her transparency was embarrassing. I looked at Cora, who semi-grinned at me condescendingly and slowly shook her head. She clearly knew the rumours. In my mind she was responsible for igniting them; top of the suspects' list. I glanced at Rosie. Her face suggested a different expression

179

altogether. Ashen would be the only word to describe it. And, unlike Cora, this look wasn't a result of Miss Croal's little performance. I mouthed, are you okay? She didn't say anything, but I could sense she was itching to say something to me. She had a weight on her chest. She flicked her eyes towards the door. Meaning let's go. I flashed mine towards Miss Croal before raising my eyebrows to indicate that I was temporarily stuck.

'Miss, can I go to the toilet?' Rosie suddenly said. She was sending out a clear message to me. An invitation to meet her outside the class.

'You've just come back from your break, Rosie.'

'Please, Miss, I have to.'

'I won't budge, the answer's no.' Rosie's face was scathing.

'It's women's problems, Miss,' Rosie said. This was always the trump card for female students to play. Sometimes male students resented them for using their bodies to abuse the system. Jealousy. No teacher in their right mind could, or would, deny any female student who claimed to have 'women's problems' a toilet visit. And in half the cases for 'women's problems' read 'cigarette break'. But what can be done? They have the toilet break system by the balls. If a woman has problems a woman has problems. Ipso facto. Although, the clever teachers could count the four-week cycle of each class. A bit too OCD. I think the girls should just come clean and say from the outset 'Miss/Sir, I have my period.' As opposed to the cryptic 'women's problems.' Miss Croal knew she had no ammunition left. 'Okay, Rosie. Make it quick.' Rosie leapt from her seat, taking her bag with her. My cue was

180

next. I wanted some of the dust to settle. I waited until Miss Croal was seated and composed.

'Miss, can I nip to the toilet?'

'You're kidding me, Clem, right?'

'I'm not Miss, I have to go.'

'The answer has to be no,' she said, and then returned to what she was doing. This was what I didn't want to happen.

'Miss, I'm desperate.'

'Clem, you've just had your break.'

'I know, but I didn't need to go then.'

'Let's be honest, you're bored and disinterested and you don't really need to go, do you?'

'I'm not bored. I actually like *Waiting for Godot*.'

'And isn't it a coincidence that Rosie has just asked to go as well?' Did she know about Rosie and me? She sounded disgruntled. It was time to pull out the big guns.

'Miss, I need to go.'

'You don't.'

By this time the rest of the class had raised their heads to view our exchange.

'It's men's problems, Miss.'

Laughter. A little derision from the females. A lot of agreement from the males.

'Men's problems, eh?'

'Afraid so.'

'Okay, Clem, let's hurry it up,' she said. In that moment our relationship severed. I was reduced to being viewed in the same category as the rest of the minions. She should have realised that, at the end of the day, we are all young people: still learning, growing, carting around our own insecurities and pecularities, making a barrage of mistakes along the way. All still emotionally growing. I liked Miss Croal, however, and scalded myself for putting her in this position. This public capitulation. This public humiliation. And all because of my juvenile problems. It would be best to try and explain it all to her at a later date I thought as I slung my bag over my shoulder and headed for the 'toilets.' I hadn't returned to school for this reason, to leave classes, be a distraction. I didn't want to cause anyone any trouble. That was the last thing I wanted to do. Keep the head down, get the exams done successfully and get the hell out of dodge. That's the mantra. I mean, how hard could that have been? I placed *Waiting for Godot* on her desk and we glanced at each other. Hers was more of a glare.

'Sorry, Miss,' I whispered.

'Just go.' I think she recognised that I was in some sort of trouble and by using the word *just* in a way gave her consent to my leaving, knowing full well that I wouldn't be back.

The Boy Who Made it Rain

There was no one to be seen. The corridors were empty, so much so that the echo of my shoes could be clearly heard as I walked, first one way and then the other, in search of Rosie. There was a distinct air of *High Noon* about wandering these halls alone. Were eyes on me? Was I being followed? Had a plan already been hatched? Was I being duped and betrayed by Rosie? Did Rosie actually have women's problems? If so, it must have come on her that morning. With this on my mind I made my way to the female toilets. No noise heard from inside. Should I go in? I waited outside for a minute or so, until a second- or third-year girl came ambling along.

'Are you going to the toilet?' Stupid question.

'Naw, am aff tae confession, where dae ye think am goin?'

'Can you see if Rosie Farrell's in there for me?'

'Wit, ir you some sort ay perv?'

'Don't talk crap,' I said, trying to act all blasé.

'You're that Inglish guy, irin't ye?'

'Can you just see if Rosie is in there for me, please?'

'Ah heard that you were shaggin that inglish teechur.'

'Just find out if she's in there.'

'She's no.'

'How do you know? You haven't even looked.'

'These ir the fird- and fourff-year bogs, she'd be up at the fiff- and six-year wans.'

'Cheers, thanks for the help.'

'I won't tell everybody you hang aboot the girls' bogs.'

'Go ahead, I don't give a damn,' I said and bolted up to the senior girls' toilets, which were situated next to the smokers. Convenient. Add perversion to the litany of other things. I honestly couldn't have cared less.

'Rosie!' Silence. Pause. 'Rosie!' Silence. Pause. One last time. 'Rosie!' Nothing. I decided to enter. Tentatively. See how the other half piss. Four doors faced me. **Croals Gagging For Her Hole!!!** was written in big red letters on the first. I slowly pushed it open. Empty. It had the mark of Cora Kelly written all over it. Poor punctuation. **All Guy's Are Dicks!!!** was scribbled on the next door I tried. Once again empty. No idea who had written it, but whoever it was needed to brush up on their grammar and punctuation too. The third door made me smile. Someone had written **Fuck** above **The Fratellis,** below which was scrawled **The Smiths Will Save Your Soul!!** Written by the fair hand of Rosie. Made me feel all empowered. Nice to see no mistakes also. I didn't make it to the final door because the next thing I know the main door had swung open. Panic. I shot into the third cubicle and closed the door behind me. Facing the toilet as opposed to sitting on it. I stood there as still as I could. Like a game of statues. The only thing I couldn't restrain were my hands, which, out of fear, shook uncontrollably. My feet glued to the floor. It was as if rigor mortis had set in. This had the potential for disaster. It did occur to me that it could be Rosie, but whoever it was didn't have the same movement as Rosie, nor did they make the same idiosyncratic sounds as Rosie, their shoes clicked off the floor too. Rosie wore trainers. Red vintage *Diadora*. Nothing with a heel. Ever. My face remained in its contorted expression, becoming even more twisted when the visitor clicked the lock to close the cubicle next to mine. I heard the knickers being taken down.

Please don't be a shit. I said it over and over in my head. The pssssshhhhh sound was a welcome friend – still disconcerting but a welcome sound nevertheless – but I still waited for the aftermath. A beat. More liquid. Relief. If that girl had any idea I was standing in the next cubicle listening to her I'd be finished. Dropped from a great height. Expulsion with honours. All it would take for her to run screaming down the corridors was a peak over or the instigation of a conversation. Who knows what she would have accused me of? Touching her? Wanking off? This was a bastard situation. I'd be unceremoniously escorted off the school premises. Blanket over the head. I stopped breathing in case she sensed that someone was next to her. In case she sensed it was male breathing. The pssssshhhhh sound ceased, the knickers were pulled up and the door was unlocked. I exhaled out of my nose. Relieved. She failed to wash her hands and left humming *Wonderwall*. I shifted my feet and pirouetted around **For A GOBBLE...Ask Cora!!!** covered the majority of the door. Poor Cora. I just couldn't feel any sympathy, however. After my hands stopped shaking I slid back the lock and made a quick exit. Hoping that no one would see me.

Where the hell was that girl and what did she have to tell me? She certainly did have women's problems alright! I was standing there outside the senior girls loos weighing up the options of where to find her. The common room was out of bounds for us, all the sniping, bitching and back biting that went on in there never sat well with Rosie and me. All you had to do was leave some group's conversation and your ears would be burning by the time you'd said your last goodbyes. Everyone was accountable. Above all else, the chat was usually inane garbage: Who was shagging who? Who was not shagging who? Who would like to shag who? Who's on Facebook? It was all extremely tiresome and tedious. What irked me most of all was whenever I entered the common room the noise level in the place receded somewhat. It made me paranoid. Rosie and I made a pact of staying away from it. She would have adhered to that pact. That was the type of girl she was. Could she have returned to class? There was no way I was going back into the English class, couldn't be bothered with the hassle. The smokers.

The smokers was a grotty little enclave close to the science classes at the very back of the school. In fact the area had two names. One was the smokers, for obvious reasons; sometimes there could be as many as fifty people there puffing away in unison, including some of the teachers: those insufferable *trendy* ones. It was also known as the groggers because it was an unwritten rule that if any first- or second-year kid dared enter that little patch of hallowed ground, they would be met with a barrage of spittle. Needless to say the vast majority of them stayed away. Those lucky enough to be authorised entry, feeding off the cigarette dregs of senior students, were either relatives of NEDs, or apprentice NEDs themselves. It didn't take an expert to know that the smokers was no place to go for those who didn't partake. And certainly no place for me. Rosie went on the odd occasion to keep Cora company.

186

However, I'm pretty sure she sneaked the odd drag or ten, even though she told me otherwise. I thought I'd pop my head outside there just to make sure.

I could see one half of the smokers from the little rectangular windows in the door. The ground was littered with hundreds of cigarette butts, and that was just in one morning. The janitors usually cleaned it up every day. An exercise in futility. No one to be seen. I opened the door. Stepped outside.

Godot!

'Well, look wit the fuckin cat dragged in.' McEvoy was standing with one of his legions. A scrawny little runt of a guy, hair matted with gel and pulled down over his forehead. I'd never laid eyes on him before. He must have been an outsider. An infiltrator. Immediately I didn't trust him. His face looked as though it had been set on fire and put out with a golf shoe. Battle weary. Of course both lads were dressed in the standard attire: the shell suit.

'How are you, Fran? I'm actually looking for Rosie,' I said. By this time Fire Face had run up, placed himself between the door and me. There was no way to turn. I was cornered. It was time to put the plan into action. Not a plan as such, more of a plea.

'Have you seen her?'

'Wit did ah tell you aboot comin back in tae ma school?' He edged closer. As did Fire Face behind me. I could smell him on me. A mixture of smoke, hash and B.O. McEvoy took a long drag of his joint. 'Eh, wit did ah tell ye, ya Inglish cunt?'

'Look can we not talk about this, Fran?'

'Answer the question cunt.'

'I don't understand what I've done…'

'…Answer the fuckin question bawbag,' he said, taking a step closer. My legs were shaking with fear. Every part of my body was sweating. My periphery narrowed as everything focussed on this one figure standing three feet in front of me. 'Waant some ay this wee man?' he asked Fire Face before passing the joint to him. Fire Face reached out from around me and snatched it from him. That was my moment to bolt. They were off guard. I'd out run them, no problem. I was fit. I had endurance. Fucking Rosie.

'Look Fran, I don't want any trouble.'

'Well you've come tae the wrang fuckin place.'

'Do him, Fran,' Fire Face said, with a disconcerting amount of exhilaration in his voice. I turned to look at him. 'Wit ir you lookin it ya fud?'

'Ah telt ye ye'd git ripped, didn't ah?' McEvoy said.

'Chib the cunt,' Fire Face said. He was riling me more than McEvoy.

'For what reason?' I asked. I felt the top of my thigh. My insurance. My madness.

'Coz yer an Inglish cunt.'

'That's it?'

'Aye.'

'So you're going to jeopardise your freedom just because I'm English.'

'Nae cunt ill know.'

'They will, because I'll tell them.'

'An if ye dae that a'll fuckin dae ye right in, if ye know wit ah mean.'

'Well you'll have to do that now. Right here and now.' I was trying to call his bluff, confuse him, stall him, anything. At very least hoping that someone would pop out for their half-hourly hit. Where were those insufferable teachers when you needed them most?

'Wit ir ye talking aboot, ya fanny?' McEvoy said.

'You'll have to 'dae me in' here and now because if you come anywhere near me, I will tell anyone who'll listen that I was attacked by Fran McEvoy.'

'Oh will ye now?'

'I will.'

'Fuckin stab the cunt, Fran,' Fire Face shouted. I could sense that McEvoy was in a quandary about what to do. If it were just the two of us in the smokers I'm sure he would have backed down. But because this little runt was present, coming between us, he couldn't be seen to back down. He couldn't relent. He had to save face, if not, word would have spread like wildfire among the NEDs, which could mean losing his title and position as number one alpha-NED. It was a shit situation for us all.

'Slash the prick,' Fire Face shouted.

McEvoy was feeling the pressure. Both of us were backing him into different corners now. He stares at me with piercing eyes, places his right hand into his side jacket pocket of his shell suit and whips it out. A knife. A blade. A cutter. I saw the shine. The glint. The sparkle. The length of a middle finger. Just enough length to pierce an artery or puncture a lung or perforate a kidney or burst a heart or prick an eye or nick a brain or slice a cheek or open a face. This was the moment that I could end up having my very own fire face. I felt again for my insurance. Still in place.

From behind, Fire Face made a grab for my arms. My strength held him off. Or, was it anticipation? Ninja Boy! I was too quick for him. All that rugby had paid off. As I span around I smacked him flush on the nose with my fist. At first I wasn't sure if the loud crack was his nose exploding or was it his jaw? Cheekbone? He plummeted to the ground. During his journey down my knee rose, connected with the crown, wham! Another crack.

Very quick.

Very sharp.

Very sore.

Take no prisoners.

He writhed about on the ground moaning.

Lots of blood.

Lots of agony.

Fee Fi Fo Fum I smell the blood of a Scotsman, with a broken nose and possibly a broken jaw. Or fractured cheekbone.

Moaning. I'm looking at him, down at him, feeling this

190

huge surge of anger rise from within me, anger at the guy who seconds earlier was baying for my blood, who was willing McEvoy to stab me. Egging him on. Chib the cunt, would you? Boiling water. The tipping point. This little prick would get my kick. Again and again and again. Head, stomach, ribs I'm not one hundred percent sure. All of them and more. And more. I was following my feet. One two three. Kick. Boot. McEvoy watches. Out comes the insurance. Surreptitiously. Last resort, I'd reminded myself.

OUCH!

One two three.

Kick.

Boot.

OUCH!

OUCH!

OUCH!

No more moaning. McEvoy static. Staring. Magnet shoes on. Stuck. Or so I believe. Never underestimate a fool.

McEvoy is on me.

Pounced.

Disgruntled cat.

He's heavier than I'd given him credit for. A pain in my back. Winded. More than that. Much more than being winded. Couldn't breath. Struggling to get air into my lungs. To fill them up. To get this cat-like monkey off my back. The knees buckling. Sweat. Getting hotter. Getting colder.

Punches. Fists. Slaps. Hotter. Colder. Reining in on the back of my head, on the cheek, on the eye. Another bastard bruise. On the same eye. The other eye. The good one. Two bastard-bruised eyes. I'm a boxer now. A prize fighter. Blood running out of the nose. Eyes streaming. Can't get him off. Swinging, slinging trying every move in my repertoire. Catman. Claws penetrating my skin. Use your insurance. I can feel the

drip

drip

drip

of the

blood

blood

blood.

The nose exploding. The neck stiff. Fuck, he might break my neck. He might have seen that thing they do in films. One sharp twist. Flip. Snap. Broken. Dead. It's so easy. He's a clinger. Time for the madness. He's saying stuff to me. Stuff I don't understand. Two cats fighting. One cat winning. One cat hanging on. Where is his weapon? Where is my cut? Where is the hole? The gash. The blood. The chill. The ambulance. The lights. The doctors. The parents. The prognosis. The tears. The heartache. The campaign. The funeral. The remembrance. The agony. The depression. The guilty. The repentant. Where is everyone else? Spit hits my ear. His spit. Infected spit? I try to punch him from over my head. Useless. I hit the top of his head. Hard gel. No power. Useless. This is it. The mind is resigned. The body is weak. The knees buckled. This is it. This is how it's to be. How my life has been mapped out for me. Just bloody well take it and no backchat, Clem. A white light. Slow motion. Peace. A tranquil place. I'm at home here. Good old rugger days.

Bang!

Bang!

Bang!

Still they come down. Hard rain. Thoughts of Bob Dylan. I'm making it rain. The boy who made it rain. The head is hot. Blood. I can smell it. This is it. It's like what *The Doors* sang about. Yanking. Doing a yanking thing now. Clothes ripped. Shirt exposing nipple. Youthful chest hair. Fluff. Caveman outfit. Funny thoughts through my mind: how will I get home in this state? Time for the insurance, it's now or never. Could I borrow a t-shirt from the drama class? What's for lunch? How will I explain this to Miss Croal? Will mum and dad even notice? Will the school inform them to buy me a new uniform? On knees. Looking at Fire Face. His eyes closed. Peaceful. Snoozing or...? My doing. *His* doing. McEvoy needs rain. Tired punches. Slaps only. Three punches.

Bang!

Bang!

Bang!

Nothing. Slap. Dizziness. Stars. Ringing. Madness. Nothing left except a swing with the insurance. A swing. Or was it a lunge? A rapid prod? A little poke?

193

Then a pause.

A long pause.

An eerie pause.

McEvoy falls beside me.

Over me actually. I push him off like a rag doll. No longer a cat. A ragdoll. *Bagpuss.* Motionless and pathetic. Ugly. My blood all over him. Saturated.

My blood?

Whose blood?

I'm alert. The colour of danger. Punctured in the side. Stitches job.

My blood?

McEvoy lies still.

Still.

A waterfall from his neck. Should I stop it? Pressure it? Do nought? Let the juice drain from him. Let him lick it. Breathing. Not mine. Not Fire Face. Not McEvoy. They demanded rain.

Tears. Not ours.

I turn at last.

Behind me.

My neck sore.

I turn.

I turn and see her.

At last!

At last, I found her.

And here she is.

She is here.

With me.

Looking out for me.

My guardian angel.

Art supply item in hand. A true artist. A Van Gogh gone tits up.

She's standing there.

Staring.

Ice woman.

I recall our art shop jaunt.

The insurance clenched tightly in my hand. Freshly rammed into McEvoy's jugular.

Now in the correct hand.

Staring.

Into McEvoy's jugular.

She stares at the madness. The insurance.

She recognises it.

Her mother's.

Theirs. For tomatoes, cucumbers, chicken, peppers, mushrooms, bananas and now jugulars. *How the fuck did he get his murdering hands on my knife?* That's what she's thinking… maybe. It's swirling around in her head. *That morning. He was in the kitchen for ages while I was upstairs listening to The Stone Roses. He blagged it then. He must have.*

'He was going to kill me,' I said. Shaking. A bit scared. An understatement.

'Clem, the knife,' Rosie said.

'I took it this morning, sorry. I was terrified. You can have it back. I don't need it anymore.' My eyes were on McEvoy's lifeless body.

'Oh Clem, what the fuck have you done?'

'I was looking for you. I couldn't find you.' Eyes still fixed on McEvoy. Blood still pissing out.

'This is madness,' she said. I took my eyes away from McEvoy.

'Where did you go, I was looking for you?' I asked.

'I had women's problems.'

'I couldn't find you, Rosie.'

'Clem, you need to lose that knife,' she said; I think. The trance state had found me.

'Why did you leave me in that class?'

'I told you, Clem.'

'What? Tell me, I don't understand.'

'I had women's problems.'

Sparkling Books

Vitali Vitaliev, *Granny Yaga*

Luke Hollands, *Peregrine Harker and the Black Death*

Sally Spedding, *Malediction*

Sally Spedding, *Cold Remains*

Anna Cuffaro, *Gatwick Bear and the Secret Plans*

Daniele Cuffaro, *American Myths in Post-9/11 Music*

Nikki Dudley, *Ellipsis*

David Kauders, *The Greatest Crash: How contradictory policies are sinking the global economy*

Amanda Sington-Williams, *The Eloquence of Desire*

Gustav le Bon, *Psychology of Crowds*

Carlo Goldoni, *Il vero amico (The True Friend)*

For further Revivals and more information visit:

www.sparklingbooks.com

Sparkling Books